Diary of a Teenage Girl

Chloe Book Nº. 4

face the music

a novel

MELODY CARLSON

Multnomah® Publishers
Sisters, Oregon

FACE THE MUSIC
published by Multnomah Publishers, Inc.,
and in association with the literary agency of Sara A. Fortenberry

© 2004 by Carlson Management Co., Inc.
International Standard Book Number: 1-59052-241-9

Cover design by David Carlson Design
Cover image by Dan Stone/Getty Images

Scripture quotations are from:
The Holy Bible, New International Version
© 1973, 1984 by International Bible Society,
used by permission of Zondervan Publishing House
The Holy Bible, New King James Version
© 1984, 1990 by Thomas Nelson, Inc.

Multnomah is a trademark of Multnomah Publishers, Inc.,
and is registered in the U.S. Patent and Trademark Office.
The colophon is a trademark of Multnomah Publishers, Inc.

Printed in the United States of America

For information:
MULTNOMAH PUBLISHERS, INC.
POST OFFICE BOX 1720
SISTERS, OREGON 97759

04 05 06 07 08 09 10—10 9 8 7 6 5 4 3 2 1 0

It's My Life

"This book inspired me to persevere through all my hardships and struggles, but it also brought me to the reality that even through my flaws, God can make Himself known in a powerful, life-changing way."—MEGHAN

"This book is unbelievable... It's so absolutely real to any teenage girl who is going through the tribulations of how to follow God. I've just recently found my path to God, and I can relate to Caitlin in many ways—it's a powerful thing."—EMILY

"I loved it!! It was so inspirational and even convicted me to have a stronger relationship with Christ. Thanks, Melody, this is the series I've been waiting for!!!"—SARAH

Becoming Me

"As I read this book, I laughed, cried, and smiled right along with Caitlin. It inspired me to keep my own journal. It changed my life forever. Thank you."—RACHEL

"I love all of the books! I could read them over and over!!!"—ASHLEY

"I couldn't put it down. When I was finished, I couldn't wait to get the second one!"—BETHANY

One

Tuesday, April 5

We finally finished recording our second CD, and now it's in the hands of the production experts at Omega. Their plan is to layer in some more instruments and then edit it and do all that technical stuff that's supposed to make it really rock. Or so they say. I'm not so sure myself. I actually asked Eric Green if we could just have it produced like last time (sort of down and dirty). But he just laughed. Not in a mean way, of course, but as if he thought I didn't get it.

Okay, I realize that our first CD might not have had the best quality and everything, but I do think that album has a very cool feeling to it. Kind of funky and natural and not overly mixed. But no, that's not good enough anymore. Now that Redemption has managed to hit the top twenty list, Eric says, "We've got to raise the bar, girls." Oh well, what do I know?

But at least we're "on the road again" (as famous old songwriter, Willie Nelson, so aptly put it long ago). And it feels pretty good to be back in our bus and have the old road whizzing beneath the tires on our way down south to sunny

Florida. Although it's not actually the same bus as before, which was a bit disappointing, at least to me. This bus is supposed to be superior, with a bigger engine and more room. Mostly it's just a lot fancier with its Italian tile floors and exotic wood cabinets. But Allie and Laura both think it's pretty cool. They like the flat-screen TV, extra appliances, and the new "designer" color scheme. However, I sort of miss the old one. I think it had more personality and didn't smell so new. Of course, I don't mention this to anyone. I don't think they'd get it.

At least Omega let us have our old driver. We were all pretty jazzed to see Rosy back behind the wheel. It's like our little "band family" is back together again. Like a reunion tour. Well, sort of.

It was impressive how quickly we all fell into our old routines—doing our schoolwork in the mornings, practice time in the afternoons, and just hanging out or watching old movies on nights we don't perform.

Even Allie's little brother, Davie, seems to have settled in fairly well. And if you ask me, that kid is really smart. I mean, in his own special way. I realize that Down's syndrome has to do with intelligence and learning abilities, but Davie seems to have some really caring instincts that the rest of us haven't developed. Like when he comes up and gives you a hug just when you need it most. In a way he seems like a little walking miracle. And it was fun to see how excited he was when we all were back together on the bus again. He calls it the "Happy Bus." All in all, our transition was much smoother this time.

And Laura was totally cool about everything. No homesickness, anxiety attacks, or general moping around. And so far, Elise hasn't had to nag us too much about doing our schoolwork. I think being back in school was a good reminder that our education is still a pretty serious deal. None of us, especially Laura since she plans to graduate in June, want to see our grades dropping in the last semester before summer break.

There's only one small problem (or potential problem), and I may just be imagining things. But I'm pretty sure that Willy is falling for Elise. I've suspected this for quite a while, but lately it seems fairly obvious. At least to me. I've seen him watching her with this kind of starry-eyed gaze lately. He's always helping her with Davie, and he loads and unloads her bags from the bus first, and he seems to be really interested whenever she says anything, even if it's something like: "We need to stop at the Quickie Mart and get some milk today." It's actually rather sweet to imagine that two somewhat lonely people, like Willy and Elise, could find romance at this stage of life.

Not that they're so old. Anyway, Elise isn't. According to Allie, she's in her midthirties. But I'm guessing Willy is a lot older. Maybe even close to fifty. Although he's got a young spirit.

Still, their little romance, if you could call it that, might pose a problem for us. Mainly because Willy is our manager and Elise is our chaperone, and I'm not sure how someone like, say, Laura's mother would feel if she thought the two of them were getting romantically involved. She might even decide to pull the plug on this whole tour or something equally extreme. Especially since it wasn't easy to get her to agree to allow Laura to come back on tour in the first place. It's like we really need to play our cards right on this trip.

Okay, I'm probably sounding pretty selfish right now, not to mention slightly paranoid. Like all I care about is keeping our little concert tour on track. And maybe that's true. After all, we do have a contract to fulfill, and Omega's got a lot of bucks riding on this spring tour. Not only are we opening for Iron Cross, but we are the main event in a number of towns as well. Eric Green says that Redemption has, or almost has, arrived.

Anyway, I guess I don't want to see anyone or anything mess us up this time. So I'm really praying that God will be in control of this whole Willy and Elise thing. Meanwhile, it is reassuring to know that they're both strong Christians and would never do anything stupid to jeopardize this tour. Besides, for all I know, Elise may not have the slightest romantic interest in Willy. Come to think of it, she sure doesn't act very interested. Although I think it's hard to tell with grown-ups sometimes. Come to think of it, I may just be imagining the whole crazy thing.

Okay, speaking of romance, I must confess (at least to this page) that I am really looking forward to seeing Jeremy Baxter again. And I'm sure that's an understatement since I seem to be thinking about him almost constantly. Oh, I'm not stupid. I'm fully aware that there's nothing going on between him and me, but I suppose I like to imagine there could be. And who knows, maybe someday there will be. Although I've heard that relationships within the music industry can be pretty tricky at best. Especially when it's two lead performers from two different bands. But maybe that could work in our favor too. Maybe we'll just get to continue being good friends for the next year or so, until I have time to grow up (or become eighteen, whichever comes first). Maybe by then I'll be taken more seriously by him.

Not that he doesn't take me seriously, exactly. He does. Well, sort of. At least he seems to take me seriously when we're talking about music or songwriting or performing or recording or God. We've had some very cool conversations about God. But on the other level (the boy-girl getting involved romantically level), it feels as if he still regards me as just his goofy kid sister, which I suppose only makes sense. After all, he's about the same age as my older brother Josh. And that's sort of how Josh treats me—like he still likes to do that rough-up-the-hair routine or relentlessly tease me when he knows I'm in a grumped-out mood.

And in some ways it seems Jeremy is no different than Josh in this regard. However, I like to imagine that it's his way of keeping this invisible line between us—like if he didn't, well, who knows what might happen? But I suppose it's just the way life is, and I shouldn't go around making it into something it's not. It's probably for the best that he's the big grown-up and I'm just the little kid. Or at least in his eyes. I sure don't feel much like a little kid myself. Well, mostly I don't. Although I sometimes wonder when I grew up and how it happened so fast. I think I sort of consider myself an adult since I'm already involved in what's looking to be a pretty successful career. Not only that, but I feel kind of responsible for Allie and Laura. I know that sounds pretty ridiculous, and I would never admit as much to them, but I feel like I sort of got us all into this crazy trip, and if it goes badly it'll be my fault.

But when it comes to Jeremy, things change. And I suppose I get to play the little kid, kid sister, or whatever. And maybe it's a good act because I think it helps to keep my heart in line. Because, otherwise...well, who knows? But hey, I can still dream, can't I?

Besides, I'm not the only dreamer around here. Allie is getting pretty psyched about seeing Brett James (gorgeous drummer from Iron Cross) again. Just this morning she got this crazy idea about inviting him to Harrison High's prom next month. I mean, what's up with that?

"Can you imagine how cool it would be to show up at the prom with someone like Brett by my side?" Then Allie let out this dreamy sigh that sounded like something right out of the old beach movie we watched last night with Annette FunnyJello, or whatever her name is, starring with that other beach dude.

"I wouldn't get my hopes up, Al," I warned her, being my usual careful and somewhat skeptical self.

"Why not?" she insisted. "Brett's just a regular guy. And during our last tour, he mentioned how he missed out on a lot of the high school stuff because Iron Cross was getting so popular around then."

"You honestly think he'd come to our prom?"

"Yeah. And I think he'd have a good time too."

I couldn't help but laugh at this. "You really think Brett James would have a good time at our small-town, Podunk prom?"

Then she punched me in the arm. "Quit making fun of me, Chloe!"

"I'm not making fun of you. Just doing a little reality check. I mean, really, don't you think it's a little far-fetched?"

She made her you-just-don't-get-it face, then in an uppity voice said, "You'll see."

"Can't wait." I turned back to my schoolwork.

"And don't get all bent out of shape and jealous when Laura and I both have prom dates, and you're sitting at home all by yourself watching reruns of 'Sabrina, the Teenage Witch.' "

"Oh, yeah, like I really watch that kind of stupid TV." I rolled my eyes at her, then considered the information she had just leaked out, I'm sure on purpose since I could tell she was trying to keep me going. However, Laura was back in the bedroom doing her schoolwork on the computer, so there was no way to know whether Allie was just stringing me along or not. "Are you saying Laura has a date to the prom?"

Allie nodded with raised brows, then lowered her voice. "She told me just this morning. I guess she'd e-mailed Ryan Hall a few days ago and jokingly invited him to the prom. She was pretty surprised when he e-mailed back and actually said yes. He's going to come home from college that weekend just to take her."

"You're kidding? I thought those guys were history."

"Not according to Laura. Sheesh, Chloe, don't you ever talk to her?"

"Not about that. At least not lately. Really, I thought it was over and done."

"Yeah, well, looks like it's not. She probably didn't tell you because she thought you'd rain on her parade too."

"Hey, I'm sorry, Allie. I just find it hard to believe that Brett would really want to go to the Harrison High prom."

"You'll see," she said again, rather smugly too.

I just nodded and looked down at my algebra assignment, which probably should've been about finished by now.

But Allie wasn't ready to quit. "The problem with you, Chloe," she said, hushing her voice even more since Elise was looking back from where she was sitting in the front seat next to Rosy, and it was clear that she was giving us the eye. But Allie continued anyway. "You focus too much on the music, and then you totally forget that you need to have a life too. That's what

Brett says about Jeremy, and I think it's true
with you too. Brett says they focused so much on
music that he never had a normal teenage life,
and he can never get that back and—"

"Allie." Elise used her firm voice.

She rolled her eyes at her mom. "Yeah, yeah, I
know."

At that point, I turned my attention back to
schoolwork, relieved that this increasingly
frustrating conversation had finally come to an
end, or at least a short pause.

Okay, I do realize that Allie may have a
point. It's possible, maybe even likely, that I do
get a little obsessed with music. But it's not
that I don't want to have a life. And really, I do
want to keep these things in balance. I'm just
not always sure how to go about it. I mean, here
we are on the road, doing concerts, cutting CDs,
all kinds of stuff. It's like we've been handed
this incredibly amazing opportunity to reach
people with our music—a pretty big deal if you
ask me—and I really don't want to blow that off
either.

I know, more than ever, I need to keep my eyes
on God. It's like He's the center of this precari-
ous teeter-totter that I'm sitting on—my music on
one side, my life on the other. And ultimately, He's
the only One who can keep me balanced.

BALANCING
one step left
one step right
eyes are focused
on the Light
not too fast
not too slow
step-by-step
here we go
keep your head
guard your heart
where to stop
when to start
time to run
time to rest
eyes on One
who knows me best
cm

TWO

Saturday, April 9

We're in Orlando now and today was a "free" day, meaning we only had to practice a couple of hours this morning and then got to have the rest of the day to do as we pleased. We opened a concert for Iron Cross last night, the first time we've performed with them since we started our spring tour. Eric Green and some of the bigwigs from Omega showed up to check us out. They probably wanted to see if we had really pulled ourselves back together after the whole drug thing with Laura last winter. According to Eric, we did just fine, and no one is the least bit worried.

But I wasn't so sure. I thought Redemption sounded a little weak or maybe just rusty. Anyway, there's certainly room for improvement. I told Willy as much, and for that reason he had us practice today instead of having the whole day off. I know, I know; I'm a freaked-out slave driver. But as I told Allie and Laura at breakfast, "This is a job, not a vacation. We need to take it seriously and give it all we've got."

"But the guys are all heading over to Disney World this morning," complained Allie. I knew she meant "the guys" as in the Iron Cross guys and in particular Brett. "And besides," she continued, "Eric said we sounded pretty good last night."

"Do you want to sound <u>pretty good</u> or <u>really hot</u>?" I asked her.

She frowned but didn't answer.

"Chloe's right," said Willy. "You girls sounded okay last night, but you need to really buckle down and put your hearts into it. Don't forget that Iron Cross has been performing pretty steadily while you girls have been in school and enjoying some downtime. There's definitely room to bring it up a notch or two."

Laura nodded. "I gotta agree with Willy and Chloe. If we're going to do this, we better do it all out." She pushed her empty breakfast plate away. "And I, for one, am ready to go to work."

So Allie got over her little pity party, and we actually had a really good practice and even tried out a new song I'd written a week ago. Then to Allie's delight, we packed it all up and hopped on the hotel shuttle and headed straight for Disney World. Willy and Elise and Davie came along too, but they decided to take the quieter route, so we split and promised to meet back up with them at the hotel later on tonight. Then Laura, Allie, and I stood in lots of lines and rode the wildest rides until Laura got thoroughly sick and threatened to throw up on us. We sat her down and made her drink a ginger ale and then headed over to the Epcot Center, where Allie had told the guys we might catch up with them by dinnertime.

"You really think we'll find them here amid all these thousands of people?" I asked her.

"Sure," she said with her perennial optimist's grin. "Why not?"

Then, just as we were watching the Japanese drummers (Allie, being a drummer herself, was totally spellbound by their fast-paced and physical drumming act), who should show up but the guys—all four of them.

"Hey, it's those groovin' chicks from Redemption!" shrieked Brett, as he raced over to where we were standing and acted like he wanted to get our autographs.

"No way!" said Allie. Not missing a beat, she put on her best starstruck expression herself. "Look, you guys," she cried. "It's those hottees from Iron Cross!"

Well, that was all it took to get a number of people looking our way, and before we knew what hit us, there were a handful of kids who recognized the name of not only Iron Cross, but Redemption as well. So right there in the Japanese drum section (fortunately the energetic performers were taking a much-deserved break), we had a little autographing party and even informed the kids about our upcoming concert tomorrow night in Miami. All in all, it was kind of fun, and I didn't even freak out at being slightly mobbed. I guess I have matured a little.

Then the seven of us went to dinner at a Mexican restaurant. It was good catching up with the guys' latest bits of news, and it sounded as if they'd been having a pretty solid spring tour with three albums riding the bestsellers chart, in the top five, even! But in the midst of everything, I have to admit I still felt slightly amazed by all this. I mean, how weird is it that we three ordinary girls from Harrison High are hanging with Iron Cross? Go figure! And not only are we sharing a meal, it's like we're all old buddies enjoying a happy reunion. I still need to pinch myself sometimes. Never mind that we're a band with a contract and doing a concert tour, but to be friends with the likes of Iron Cross! So cool. I know I should be over this by now, but the truth is, I still get a little starstruck sometimes. But hey, I'm only human, right?

Allie and Brett and Isaiah decided to head back to Disney World to hit some more rides, but Laura and I stayed with Jeremy and Michael. The four of us just walked around and looked at some more of the Epcot exhibits, but I thought it was kind of interesting how we sort of paired off.

Kind of like a double date. Fortunately, I got paired with Jeremy and Laura was with Michael. Okay, I realize that Laura and Michael had been discussing some new technique that Michael has been experimenting with on bass, and since Laura plays bass too, well, it's only natural she'd want to hang with him. She actually thinks Michael White is one of the best bass players on the planet. But even so, I was pretty jazzed to be hanging with Jeremy Baxter all night. He didn't seem to mind being stuck with me either.

To say it was a pretty cool evening would be a serious understatement. But at the same time, I keep telling myself to just chill and not get too serious about Jeremy. Because that could ruin everything between us. Besides, I know for a fact that practically every Christian girl in the country (at least the ones who listen to Christian music) are either in love with him or his brother, Isaiah. And I also know it's kind of silly and immature to be so stupidly smitten. I'm probably just having some sort of schoolgirl crush that will clear up eventually like a bad case of acne.

But if the truth were to be known, I really hope it's something more too. Naturally, I will tell this to no one. This is strictly a diary thing. I have no delusions here—I fully understand that God knows all about the condition of my heart. There's no keeping secrets from God.

MY HEART
an open book
for You to look
no way to hide
what lurks inside
You know me well
and You can tell
the way i feel
You know what's real
You know my heart
each hidden part
the way i long
God, is it wrong?
is it from You
what You might do?
or is it me
what i want to be?
i lay it all
the big, the small
into Your hand
You understand
amen

Friday, April 15

Well, that Allie. She went and did it. Invited
Brett to the prom last week. And guess what? She
was right. He wants to go. And even more amazing,
Iron Cross doesn't have anything scheduled that

same weekend, and he's actually available to go.
Well, who'd've thought?

"Why don't you ask Isaiah?" Allie urged me
today. The three of us had taken our lunches into
the practice room, and even though we were done
eating, Willy hadn't gotten there yet. So we were
sitting around gabbing about pretty much nothing. But then she and Laura got stuck on the
irritating subject of prom dresses. Naturally, I
tuned this out (I think I was daydreaming about
Jeremy). But I suppose they assumed that I was
feeling left out, so they immediately tried to
pull me back in with their ridiculous Isaiah
idea.

"Isaiah?" I stared at Allie as if she'd totally
lost it. "Get real."

"Hey, I happen to think he'd really like to go
with you," said Allie defensively. "I mean, he was
acting like he was all jealous after I invited
Brett the other night. Isaiah said it was totally
unfair that he didn't get to go to his prom this
year, and he's even a senior. Unfortunately, it was
the same night that we'd all performed in Tulsa."

"Too bad," I said. But the truth was, I was
thinking it was too bad that I couldn't invite
Jeremy to go to the prom with me. But then how
would that look? A seventeen-year-old girl going
to the prom with a twenty-one-year-old man! Oh,
I don't think of Jeremy that way, really. He doesn't

seem like an adult in that sense. To me he's just one of us, only a little older. But I could imagine what my parents or someone like Laura's mom might say about it. Besides that, I seriously doubt that Jeremy would agree to go with me anyway. I'm sure he'd probably think a high school prom was way beneath him . Crud, I think it's beneath me, and I'm still in high school!

"Why don't you ask him, Chloe?" urged Laura.

"Huh?" I was shocked. Had she been reading my mind about asking Jeremy to the prom?

"Like Allie suggested, why don't you invite Isaiah to the prom?" She said the words slowly as if she thought I was having a hard time following her.

But I just shook my head.

Suddenly Allie got that stubborn look in her eye. It's how she acts when she thinks she's come up with some brilliant idea, even if it's totally lame. "Come on, Chloe. It'd be fun."

"I can't ask him—"

"Yes, you can," said Laura quickly. "Allie's right about this. I heard the whole conversation the other night. It was after the Atlanta concert; you and Jeremy and Michael were still signing CDs. But Isaiah sounded really bummed that he was about to graduate from high school without attending a single prom. He said the same thing happened to him last year. In fact, I think he said that Jeremy's the only one in the band who's ever gone to a prom."

"Jeremy went to the prom?" I realized at once that I'd said this with way too much interest. I hoped my disappointment didn't show since I was really thinking, "Who'd Jeremy go to the prom with?" So I nonchalantly added, "That's funny. Jeremy doesn't seem like the prom type to me."

"I know," agreed Allie. "But I guess he has a girlfriend in his hometown. Apparently, she talked him into it when they were still in high school."

"Jeremy has a girlfriend?" I could tell my voice sounded kind of high-pitched and funny, but fortunately no one else seemed to notice.

"Yeah, that was news to us too, but Isaiah said that Jeremy's been dating the same girl for about four or five years now."

"That's almost like being engaged," added Laura, as if she was some kind of authority on these things.

"No, it's not," I said a little too quickly.

"It would be for me," Laura retorted.

"So how about it, Chloe?" pleaded Allie. "Why don't you ask Isaiah? It's not like you guys need to be involved or anything. You can just go together as friends and have a good time."

"Yeah," agreed Laura. "We could triple date. It would be so cool."

"I don't know." I was looking at the floor now, tracing the diamond pattern of the carpet with the toe of my Doc Martens.

"Just think about it," said Allie. "It's still about three weeks away."

"Yeah," I muttered. "I'll think about it." And thankfully, Willy arrived and then we started to practice. But to be honest, I had a hard time focusing on our practice, and I'm afraid it didn't go too well, which I'm sure was mostly my fault. Ironic, since I'm the one always pushing for perfection.

Finally, we finished and I told them that my stomach didn't feel too great. "I think it's something I ate." Although I knew that wasn't true. Unless you can ingest a conversation, which I suppose is sort of true. And that's sort of what it feels like. Like I swallowed a bunch of foul-tasting words. Anyway, I excused myself and went up to our room in the hotel.

I lay down on my bed and cried myself to sleep. I know it's stupid. It's not like Jeremy and I actually had anything going on, or as if he'd led me on at all. It was all just in my head. I guess that's what comes of letting your mind run wild about things like guys and romance.

Well, when I woke up, I wrote this all down in my diary. Kind of like I just needed to barf it out so I could feel better. And then I read my Bible and prayed. I've decided that I need to just pull myself together and put this whole thing into God's hands.

I can see how a girl could let something like this totally devastate her and just emotionally wipe her out for days, maybe even weeks. But I also realize that, like I've been telling Allie and Laura, we have a job to do. And we have a big concert tomorrow night where Redemption is the main event, so I really need to get my head and my heart together—for the sake of the band, our recording contract, and most of all for the audience who has paid good money to hear us. Hopefully, they'll be touched by God when they do.

So I'm making this commitment to myself and to God: I will not let this disappointment about Jeremy mess up my music. If anything, I have decided that this whole thing can just make me stronger. Like that verse I memorized in James. Maybe it will become my "life verse" since Pastor Tony says that everybody should have at least one Bible verse that they take with them through everything. Perhaps this is mine.

"...count it all joy when you fall into various trials, knowing that the testing of your faith produces patience. But let patience have its perfect work, that you may be perfect and complete, lacking nothing."

Now how cool would it be to become perfect and complete and lacking nothing? And if that comes from going through trials, well, I guess I should just say, "Bring 'em on." Okay, let's not get carried away. I'm not asking to be hit by a truck or suffer from some horrible skin disease or anything too dramatic. But I do recall Pastor Tony preaching about how we should greet our trials as we greet our friends. We should welcome them as we realize how they've come to make us bigger and better people.

BRING 'EM ON
here we go, God
bring on the crud
pour on the rain
sling on the mud
bring on the hard times
fling on the bad
bring on the tears
heap on the sad
pile it all up, Lord
it won't be long
'til all these trials
help make me strong
cm

Three

Wednesday, April 20

Is it possible that I have deceived myself into believing that God would change my personality in order to make me more acceptable to Him? Okay, I realize this sounds a bit crazy, but I'm thinking, God _did_ give me my personality (even if some people think it is a pretty weird one!). Anyway, I assume He did since He "knit me together in my mother's womb," and I figure that means He created my DNA which makes me who I am. Right? So if this is the personality He gave me, then He probably doesn't want to change it. I mean, I realize He wants me to become more like Him. But it's not like He's going to give me a spiritual lobotomy and turn me into something completely different.

So I have to ask myself—just who's doing the changing around here? I mean, people used to call me a wild child, a rebel, a nonconformist. But in some ways, I think I've been trying to conform myself. Like I thought maybe that would make God happy. Now I'm wondering whether that was God's plan? Or mine?

The reason I'm so concerned about this is

because I think it's affecting my music. And this scares me. The last thing I want is to end up sounding like everyone else, to lose my creative edge. I guess this is something I admire about Jeremy. He doesn't seem to be affected in this way. It's like he doesn't compromise who he is. He remains his own self. Oh, I didn't mean to start going on about Jeremy again. In fact, I've been doing a pretty good job of blocking my thoughts about him. Or at least I thought so.

But speaking of Jeremy, I now have a new problem. I suppose it's not fair to call Isaiah Baxter a problem. Sheesh, I know there are millions of girls who would love to have such a problem. But it seems that Allie and Laura are playing matchmaker for me. Oh, not matchmaker exactly. Rather, they are still trying to set us up to go to the prom.

"He said he wants to go with you," Laura said last night when we stopped in for a fast-food dinner after pleading with Elise. (She thinks fast food will kill you, and she's probably not far from the truth.)

"But only if you ask him yourself," added Allie. "He doesn't want a middleman."

Fortunately, we three girls were seated at our own table because I'm not sure I'd want the "grown-ups" (Willy, Rosy, Elise) listening in on our conversation. I'm not even sure why. "I don't even want to go to the prom," I told them for like the umpteenth time. "I'm not exactly a prom sort of girl, if you remember."

"Oh, come on, Chloe," said Allie. "It's not like you have to put on a pink Cinderella dress and wear pumps."

"You have a problem with pink?" demanded Laura.

"Oh, yeah," I said. "Doesn't your mom have a pink dress all picked out for you to wear to the prom?"

Laura scowled at me. "It's not so bad."

"I know." I attempted a smile on her behalf. "But the thing is, I do NOT want to go to the Harrison High prom."

"Not even with Isaiah?" asked Allie.

"Yeah," said Laura. "Now you're going to hurt his feelings."

"Hey, it's got nothing to do with Isaiah—"

"Try telling him that," said Allie.

I knew they were quickly getting me cornered between that proverbial rock and a hard place. "You guys are impossible!"

And so now I'm stuck here trying to decide what to do. Do I just go with the flow and invite Isaiah to the prom? I know it really doesn't mean anything from a romantic standpoint. I'm sure he knows that, too. Still, it feels like it must mean something. Shouldn't you go to the prom with someone you really care about? Like Jeremy? Or even Cesar? It wasn't that long ago that I would've imagined myself going to the prom with Cesar. But true to his word, the guy is still kissing dating goodbye. Well, good for him. Maybe I should do the same.

But that brings me back to my earlier question. Like who am I? I'm afraid that I've been conforming myself into what and who other people think I should be. And the only one who should be conforming me is God. Or rather transforming me. But what if I keep getting in the way?

YOUR PLAN

change me

rearrange me

but according to Your plan

make me

just don't fake me

into something i can't stand

mold me

even scold me

if it makes me more like You

fill me

Jesus, heal me

make me real and true

amen

Friday, April 22

Okay, it's a done deal. I am officially going to the prom. And yes, I am going with Isaiah. I'm not sure if it was a compromise or what. But to be honest, I don't feel bad about it, so it's probably not such a big deal. Sometimes I think I make more of something than it really is. Like I kind of blow things out of proportion in my head. Maybe that's why it's good to talk about things with your friends.

Anyway, here's how it happened. We just finished our concert in Savannah tonight, and I was heading out from the ladies' restroom, of all places, on my way out to the foyer for a little "M and S" (that's Meeting and Signing for fans seeking autographs) when I ran smack into Isaiah, also heading out from the bathroom.

"Hey," he said with a funny grin. Now why is it slightly uncomfortable to see someone of the opposite sex emerging from a restroom? Is it like we think they don't go?

So I nodded to the bathroom sign above his head. "Hey, when you gotta go, you gotta go."

He laughed. "Man, is that ever the truth. I thought I'd be standing in a puddle before our last song was even halfway finished."

Well, I suppose all this potty talk had loosened

me up and put me into a goofy mood because before I knew what hit me, I was shooting off my mouth. "I hear you wanna attend a real live high school prom."

He broke into a huge and rather handsome grin. "So the cat's outta the bag now."

"Yeah. It's hard to keep too many secrets with the crowd we hang with." We were almost to the foyer now. "But if you really want, you can come with me. It's not like the Harrison High prom is anything to brag about—"

"Hey, I'd love to come, Chloe. And it might not seem like any big deal to you, but sometimes it feels like I missed out on everything that had anything to do with high school."

"I guess I know what you mean. Still, I wouldn't trade this for—"

"Chloe Miller!" yelled a fan who'd just spotted me coming around the corner. She looked to be all of twelve and was wildly waving her shiny orange autograph book in the air. "Will you sign this for me?"

"Later," said Isaiah.

And then, as I was smiling and signing, I had to wonder what I'd gotten myself into. I even considered tracking down Isaiah and backing out, but Iron Cross had left to catch a late flight for a concert in New Orleans. Now it looks as though I won't be talking to Isaiah until next Friday, when

we meet up with them in Jackson, Mississippi.
Maybe it's just as well.

Naturally, Allie and Laura were totally
jazzed.

"What are you going to wear?" Allie demanded
as we rode back to the hotel.

I just shrugged.

"Do we all want to go together?" asked Laura
hopefully.

"You think Ryan would like that?" I asked.
"He'd kind of be odd man out."

She frowned. "I've actually been wondering if
that's the only reason he agreed to come."

"What do you mean?"

"When I told Ryan that Allie had been thinking about asking Brett from Iron Cross, well, I
think that's when he got interested in coming.
He's a big Iron Cross fan, you know."

"Oh."

"But he still likes you," Allie said with opti-
mism, as the limo pulled up to the hotel. "Doesn't
he?"

"I don't know. My brother told me that Ryan was
pretty serious with his girlfriend at college. So
much so that he got depressed when she broke up
with him last month. James warned me that Ryan
might not even be over her yet. I might just be his
rebound girl."

"Maybe Cesar and Caitlin are right," I said as

we stepped out of the limo onto the well-lit side-walk. We waited while Willy tipped the driver and climbed out of the passenger seat. He usually rides up front, which I personally think is kind of cool since he uses the opportunity to tell the driver about Jesus.

"Right about what?" asked Laura.

"You know," I said, "the whole nondating thing. Maybe it just simplifies life for everyone."

"Someone having problems with her love life again?" teased Willy.

"Yeah," Allie said with a sly grin. "Not that you would know anything about that now, would you, Willy?"

He tossed her a funny glance as he held open the hotel door for us. "You girls better hit the hay early tonight. We've got to be out of here by six in the morning."

We all made the appropriate groaning noises as we rode the elevator up to the eleventh floor. But I did feel kind of sorry for Willy. I know that he's got it bad for Elise, but he never actually says anything. Neither does Elise. And for Allie to tease him like that just makes everyone feel uncomfortable. I may say something to her about it tomorrow. But not while anyone else is around. I've learned enough about confronting people by now to know that you should do it privately and in love.

HONEST LOVE
speak the truth
one on one
don't let anger
outshine the sun
words that hurt
won't always heal
truth with love
is the real deal
don't keep feelings
on a shelf
love your friends
as you love yourself
cm

Four

Thursday, April 28

I really like the way Eugene Peterson translates 1 Corinthians 13 (the love chapter) in "The Message." He says things like, love doesn't get a big head or strut. How cool is that? Anyway, it's inspired me to write my own version.

- Love runs a marathon with blistered heels just to keep you company.
- Love won't take a break until you have what you need.
- Love doesn't get grumpy when you win the lottery but refuse to share a penny.
- Love doesn't act like you're a stranger just because you've got a big green booger in your nose.
- Love, though perfect, isn't full of itself.
- Love doesn't push its way into places where it's not invited.
- Love never takes cuts in front of anyone.
- Love doesn't freak when you total the car.
- Love doesn't keep track of every single time you blow it.

- Love doesn't laugh when a jerk falls on his face.
- Love doesn't make the story bigger than it really is.
- Love can be spat upon, beaten, and murdered and still keep on loving.
- Love trusts God implicitly.
- Love sees the good in you even when you're acting like a total loser.
- Love doesn't feel bad about what happened yesterday.
- Love keeps running the marathon until it reaches the finish line.

Wow, now that I think about it, I think Love is really just another name for Jesus. Amazing. I'm going to make a copy of this list and keep it with me to check on from time to time, like when I'm feeling particularly impatient or grumpy or just generally out of sorts. It'll be a good reminder for me to just lighten up.

Friday, April 29

"I hear you kids are all going to the prom together," Jeremy said to me after the concert tonight. The two of us were already starting to pack things up offstage. As usual, the rest of them were still out there gabbing with the fans.

Something about the way he said "kids" kind of aggravated me, like he saw us as a bunch of toddlers playing in the sandbox together. As a result, I felt seriously irked. But then I reminded myself that Love doesn't react like that.

"Yeah," I said calmly. "Isaiah really wanted to go to a prom, and Allie and Laura talked me into it."

"Sounds like fun." He smiled as he snapped his guitar case closed. "I still remember my prom."

"You went to the prom?" I said, instantly feeling stupid and false since I already knew this bit of information. What a hypocrite I can be sometimes. Still, I wanted to hear his version—and hopefully he'd mention the mysterious girlfriend as well.

He nodded. "Yep. It was about five years ago as I recall. I think we'd just signed our first recording contract."

"But you still had time to go to prom?" I wanted to keep him talking, extracting as much information as possible.

"I probably wouldn't have gone, but I'd promised my girlfriend before we'd signed the contract. And even though it was inconvenient, I wanted to be true to my word."

"Girlfriend?" I said in a teasing tone, instantly regretting this too. What was wrong with me?

He laughed. "Yeah, even we famous rock stars are allowed to have girlfriends."

"So, are you still going with her?" I diverted my eyes from his as I pretended to focus on stacking some sheets of music.

"Yeah, but it's kind of tricky."

"Tricky?"

"You know, dating someone while you're almost constantly on tour. It's not the best for maintaining a good relationship."

"What's she like?" I asked, no longer concerned that I probably appeared overly interested as I shamelessly attempted to pry out all the varied details of his personal life. By then I was telling myself, "Hey, he thinks of me as the kid sister here." And "These are just the kind of questions I would ask Josh about him and Caitlin."

"She's a very sweet Christian girl," he told me. "She's about to graduate from Bible school with her teaching degree. She really loves kids and wants to get a job in an inner city."

"That's cool." By now the others were starting to trickle in, and I no longer had any desire for Jeremy to go on about his love life.

"Hey, Chloe," Isaiah said with a friendly smile. "Am I supposed to wear a tux to the prom or not? Laura says yea, but Allie says nay. What says ye?"

I shrugged. "I guess I don't really know."

"Is this about the tux again?" Allie said as she came backstage. "Brett and I plan to go casual—"

"But it's a prom," Laura insisted as she and Willy joined us. "You're supposed to get dressed up."

And so it went. Finally Allie and I won by majority and pure stubbornness, and it was decided that our foursome was definitely going casual. Retro even. "But you can dress however you like," said Allie nonchalantly.

"And hey, if you don't want to be seen with us—"

"No, it's okay," Laura said in a sober tone. "Maybe my mom can return the dress since it's never been worn."

I had to control myself from cheering out loud about this. Now, I don't mean to be disrespectful of Mrs. Mitchell, but sometimes it seems as though she's a little too controlling of Laura's life. On the other hand, I guess it's understandable after the way things have gone with Laura's older sister, Christine. Still, parents should know that they can't really control their kids. Shouldn't they? Man, I sure don't look forward to ever becoming a parent. I think I'll probably wait until I'm about forty before having any kids. And be married first, of course. It's just as well since I don't think that's going to happen anytime soon.

Anyway, to finish up the what-to-wear-to-the-prom dilemma, Allie came up with a brilliant solution, which we're all hoping will work out.

"Why don't we hire our personal designer?" she said suddenly. "She could coordinate all our outfits."

"You guys have a personal designer?" said Michael, obviously impressed with our little ragtag band.

"Not exactly." I didn't want to put on false airs.

"Yes, we do," insisted Allie. "Her name is Beanie Jacobs, and she's going to work out of New York and be very famous someday."

"Cool," said Brett. "You girls always look so together. I guess I just assumed you did it all yourselves."

"Does your designer friend do guys too?" asked Isaiah hopefully.

"We can ask," offered Laura.

"I'll e-mail her tonight," said Allie.

And so we're all hoping that Beanie won't be too busy to help us out.

YOUR DESIGN
perfectly, You plan my day
seamlessly, You weave the way
You go before me and behind
creating wonders that i find

You always know what is the best
when to run and when to rest
i am Yours and You are mine
sewn together by design
cm

Five

Saturday, April 30

Beanie e-mailed Allie right back, offering to coordinate outfits for all six of us. Now all we have to do is get the guys' measurements sent off to her, and she'll meet up with us the day of the prom to hand off our outfits. We didn't give her much time, but she's certain she can pull it off anyway.

"Beanie says that she'll have to take photos of us," said Allie, reading aloud from her e-mail. "It says here, 'I need to get a lot of shots of the six of you together so I can use these as well as sketches for my final project in my textile design class. So if you all agree to that, I'd love to do this. And if you don't mind, I'd like to do a retro fifties thing. Let me know. Love, Beanie.'"

"That's great," said Laura.

"Really?" I asked. "You're okay with this?"

"Yeah. My mom might actually like that it's fifties retro. She's always saying that's one of her favorite eras for clothes."

"But your mom's not that old."

"I know. She just likes it."

So it's settled. But to be honest, I'm not that

thrilled about this whole fifties thing and am frankly surprised that someone as cool as Beanie would even suggest it. I can't really see myself in a pastel-colored dress with a tight waist and full skirt, not to mention those spiky high heels. I mean, my spiky hair is one thing, but shoes? Give me a break.

Well, at least the guys seem to like it, or so Allie informed us after e-mailing Brett with the news. I think they're just relieved that someone else is handling the clothes issue for them. Allie said they refused to give her their measurements, but e-mailed them directly to Beanie instead. Allie suggested we might bribe her for this information. Yeah, sure! Anyway, I suppose I'm actually getting into this whole prom thing after all. And in a way, I guess I'm getting into Isaiah too. I mean he's not Jeremy, but he's not exactly chopped liver either!

Naturally, Allie (the love cupid) is trying to make more of this than it really is. Exactly what I was afraid of in the first place. Since she's madly in love with Brett it only makes sense to her that I should fall head over heels for Isaiah. But today I had to tell her to lay off. Privately, of course. Even so, she got mad.

"Man, Chloe, what are you becoming anyway? The mind control police? First you're on my case for saying that thing to Willy about his love life, which by the way, I did apologize for and he told me was absolutely no biggie."

"I didn't tell you that so you'd apologize to him, Allie. I just thought maybe you'd be more sensitive to his dilemma."

"His dilemma?" she shot right back at me. "For your information, he's interested in MY mother."

"I know." Suddenly I wished I'd just kept my big mouth closed.

"And how do you think it makes me feel?"

I studied her. "I don't know, Allie. How does it make you feel?"

She frowned. "To be honest, I'm not sure."

I nodded. "But you like Willy, right?"

"Of course. I mean, he's a little old, but I do think he'd make a totally cool dad. I even pretend that he is sometimes."

"So what's the problem?"

"Mainly my mom."

"Oh."

"Every single time I've asked her about it, she gets kind of upset and just closes up."

"Upset like she has absolutely no romantic interest in him and just wants you to shut up? Or upset like she likes him but it makes her uncomfortable to admit it?"

"I can't tell. But it almost makes me think she might still have feelings for my dad."

"But I thought he was remarried."

Allie rolled her eyes. "Not really. They're just 'shacking up' as my mom likes to say."

"Even so, it sounds like your dad's pretty involved with another woman."

"It seems like that to me too. I just wish my mom would get the message and move on. I mean, I love my dad and everything, despite the fact that he's been a total jerk to us, but I really wouldn't want to see Mom go back to him even if his old lady—who's actually only twenty-four—left him high and dry. I just think my mom would get hurt all over again. And I don't think I could handle that."

"Yeah, I know what you mean."

"You know what I mean?" She frowned at me with obvious skepticism. "How's that? Your parents seem pretty happily married to me."

"Okay, maybe I don't know exactly what you mean. But I can understand how it feels when someone you love is hurting over something. Whether you like it or not, you get involved, and before you know it, you're hurting too."

"Like how it was with your brother Caleb last winter?"

"Yeah, kind of like that. I mean I realize now that I can't do anything to change things for him and that he won't give up drugs until he's ready. But I still love him so much that I wish I could do something—anything. But sometimes all we can do is pray for them. Even so, it hurts."

"Okay, I guess you do get it." Allie smiled.

"Man, doesn't it just make you wish everyone was a Christian so they wouldn't mess up their lives so much?"

She nodded. "But Christians mess up too."

"But not quite as badly as others. Or maybe it's just that they go to God quicker to get fixed up."

"Doesn't it make you glad that we're doing what we're doing?" said Allie.

"Huh?" I guess I was spacing just then.

"You know, singing songs about God and telling everyone about Jesus, silly. It just might make a difference."

"Yeah." I had to laugh at myself. "You're right. God can definitely make a difference."

A DIFFERENCE
what's the difference?
what does it matter?
what's your defense?
what makes you shatter?
who really cares?
who gives a rip?
when someone shares
what made them slip?
what is the point?
what is the good
of rocking the joint?

just cuz we could
the difference is clear
between life and death
it's fleeing from fear
and feeling God's breath
it's knowing you're loved
and feeling God's grace
it's help from above
and seeing God's face
cm

Monday, May 2

My mom e-mailed me today! Man, I was pretty stunned. But I was even more surprised when reading her words made me feel like crying. I don't mean sad tears, no way. I felt like crying tears of real joy. This is what she wrote.

Hi. Chloe, your dad told me about your plans to attend the prom, and I wanted to write you personally and say how very special this is to me. I know, I know, you're probably thinking that, as usual, "Mom is only thinking of herself again." I'll admit that I am a rather self-centered person and it would thoroughly delight this somewhat superficial mother to know that her

only daughter is going to her high
school prom. But there's something
more.

As Dad has probably mentioned already,
we've been going to church more regularly
lately. This is all your fault, Chloe,
because you and your music and your
diligent commitment are making us think.
Making me think. I guess your dad's been
thinking all along. Count on me to come in
last again. Well, other than Caleb, I
suppose. But that's another story.

Suffice it to say, I am very, very proud
of you, Chloe. And I am challenged by
your life. And, yes, it's true, I'm glad that
you're going to the prom. Is that all right
for me to be happy about that? Mostly, I
just wanted to say I love you, honey.
You're the best daughter a mother could
hope for. And I'm so sorry I've been such a
lousy mom.

Well, you can just imagine that I e-mailed her
right back and assured her that she has NOT been
a lousy mom at all. Oh sure, we haven't always
seen eye to eye, but the fact is, I was a pretty
lousy daughter too. I was a totally mixed-up
mess before I let Jesus come into my life and
straighten me out. Anyway, I can't wait to see Mom

again and give her a great big hug. Oh, God is
good!!!

TRIPPING ON GOD
You are so awesome, God
the way You made me, designed my life
You are so amazing, God
amid the joy, amid the strife
You are my everything, God
You're all i want and all i see
i go tripping on You, God
i love the way You live in me
You are totally cool, God
the way You let me live Your story
You are so fantastic, God
shine through me and show Your glory
amen

Six

Tuesday, May 3

Okay, this makes absolutely no sense. But this is the deal: I think my heart is grieving. It's like I've been wearing this invisible cloak of sadness all week. I mean, I was okay about going to the prom, and I'm really happy about how things have gone with my mom. I even sent her a pretty cool Mother's Day present. But underneath all that cheerful veneer is this layer of dark gloom.

I actually thought that no one had noticed until Laura and Allie cornered me back in the bedroom on the bus today. We'd already done our schoolwork and I was hanging back there, supposedly working on a new song, but really just moping around and feeling sorry for myself because of Jeremy.

"Okay," Allie said as she flopped down on the bed next to me. "What gives?"

"Huh?"

"Come on," Laura said as she sat on the other side of me. "Tell us what's going on."

"What do you mean?" I sat up and rubbed my eyes as if I'd just woken up. I can be such a fake sometimes! Jesus, help me to be real.

"We mean why are you so bummed?" Allie peered into my eyes. "What's up?"

"Yeah, tell us what's going on with you," said Laura. "We're not just your business partners, you know, we're your friends too, remember?"

"Yeah," said Allie almost indignantly. "Sometimes you push us away, Chloe, like you don't think we'd understand anything."

"I can assure you from experience, it's not good to keep stuff bottled up inside," urged Laura. "Just tell us what's wrong. If we can't help you, we can at least pray for you."

I really didn't want to tell them what was wrong. It seemed so lame and actually kind of embarrassing. Besides, I'm the leader of this band. I'm supposed to be in charge, tuned in to God, the strong one. Right? Wrong.

"Come on, Chloe," Allie said in her sweetest voice. "Don't you know how much we love you?"

Well, that did it. Despite my best efforts, I started to cry, and before I knew what was happening, they were both hugging me and telling me it would be okay. And to my surprise, it did feel kind of good. I no longer felt so isolated and lonely. And then I just poured it all out. I told them about all about my feelings for Jeremy and how I've tried to hide it since I knew it would never work, and besides he has a girlfriend. I even told them about the jerk who broke my heart back when I was in middle school.

"I thought that was bad enough," I sobbed. "And that I'd never let it happen again. But believe me, this is way, way worse. I just don't get why I have to feel like this—so—so miserable. It's not fair."

"I know." Allie soothingly rubbed my back.

"It was total stupidity on my part." I wiped my nose on my sweatshirt sleeve. "I mean, we were only just friends, at least in his eyes, and I was trying to act like that was perfectly cool with me too. But it was just an act; I was falling deeper and deeper into it. And then, after I found out he had a girlfriend, well, I really thought I could handle this now, but it's—it's like my heart just won't listen."

"And you thought we wouldn't understand this?" said Laura kindly.

I just shrugged.

"Sheesh," exclaimed Allie. "You really should've told us sooner. Don't you know that Laura and I have way more experience in the achy breaky heart arena than you, Chloe?"

I had to smile at that.

"It's true," said Laura. "You saw me moping around about Ryan last year. Man, I was a mess. And I suppose I could be a mess again before too long." She frowned. "I mean, after the prom is over."

I nodded and put my hand on her arm. "It's weird, isn't it? Here we are trying our best to serve and follow God. We read His Word and pray regularly. We have this great music ministry where kids think we can practically walk on water, and yet, underneath it all, we're just as weak and vulnerable as every other girl out there."

"Maybe even more so," added Allie.

"How's that?" asked Laura.

"Well, maybe we have that kind of artistic temperament, you know what I mean? Where our hearts are easily pulled into things."

"Because we're passionate about our work and our lives?" I ventured.

"Yeah, and maybe that makes us more vulnerable in some ways."

"Like getting crushes on cool guys?" offered Laura.

Allie nodded.

"Wow, Al, that's pretty deep." I was actually impressed.

"I know. Sometimes I even surprise myself." She grinned.

"So, what do we do about it?" asked Laura. "I mean, I really like Ryan and everything, but I do NOT want to get all bummed if he drops me right after the prom. You know?"

"I know." I was giving this whole guy dilemma

some serious thought. It just didn't seem fair that we should be so easily derailed by a mere guy. "I have an idea."

"Yeah?" Allie looked eager.

"Well, I don't know if any of us are exactly ready to quit dating entirely, the way that Caitlin and Cesar have done."

"Don't be too sure," said Laura quickly. "I've actually been giving it some real consideration lately. And I plan on reading that book that Cesar keeps talking about."

"You mean that 'I Kissed Dating Goodbye' book?" asked Allie.

"Maybe we should all read it," I suggested. "But whether we read it or not, I'm thinking we could make a pact, just between the three of us, as a way to help keep Redemption on track and keep our hearts focused on God."

"What kind of pact?" Allie's eyes lit up as if it would be some kind of game. She always gets into stuff like this.

"Some sort of promise that says we won't allow guys to come between us and God and our ministry. Like if you're involved with Brett, Allie, and Laura and I feel that it's distracting you from God and our music, then we have the right to tell you, and you have to listen to us. Kind of what you guys did to me today."

"I like it," said Laura.

"I think I do too." Allie paused. "Although it does worry me a little. I mean, what if you think Brett is a problem, but he's really not?"

"If both Laura and I think that Brett's a problem, then I'm guessing that we're onto something. It's not like we'd be on your case for no good reason, Allie."

"Yeah. You're probably right."

"So, do you want to write something up, Chloe?" asked Laura. "Like a real pact that we can all sign and agree to?"

"Sounds good."

So this is what I wrote. We decided to have copies made, and then we'll all sign it with Willy as our witness.

THE BOYFRIEND CLAUSE

Laura Mitchell, Allie Curtis, and Chloe Miller do hereby promise to enter into the following agreement. We will NOT allow any boyfriend or romantic relationship to: 1) distract us from serving God, 2) interfere with our friendships with each other, or 3) diminish in any way our music ministry in the band known as Redemption. If one of us does not abide by this agreement, the other two signing

parties have the responsibility to
confront and encourage her to get her act
together! As God (and Willy Johnson) are
our witnesses, we do hereby agree to this
commitment.

I think it actually sounds rather legal and
binding. Not that we ever plan to take it to court,
but I do hope that we take it seriously. I think we
will. It does make me feel better to have agreed to
this pact. And I feel better to have confessed to
Allie and Laura that my heart was aching over
Jeremy. They totally understood, probably even
better than I did. After I'd spilled my guts to
them, they prayed for me, and I think that made
more difference than anything. Then they both
assured me that they'd keep on praying because
according to them, it's not easy to get over a broken heart. I think they're right. But I also
believe that God's the healer of broken hearts.

> KING OF HEARTS
> bring your hearts
> big or small
> bring your hearts
> come one and all
> bring your hearts
> broken, sad

bring your hearts
hurtin' bad
bring your hearts
to the King
who fixes them
makes them clean
the King of Hearts
can make you whole
He'll heal your heart
and mend your soul
cm

Seven

Wednesday, May 4

Now I realize that I should be very thankful that I'm going to the prom with Isaiah instead of Jeremy. Much safer for my heart. Not that Isaiah isn't a totally cool guy. He most definitely is. But for some reason it's a lot easier to be friends with him. Maybe it's because he's not so intense and serious. Of the two brothers, he's much more lighthearted and easygoing. That's probably good for me since I tend to get overly serious sometimes. But Isaiah is fun to be with, and we usually end up laughing a lot.

Does this mean I'm completely over Jeremy? Well, I wouldn't go so far as to say that. I still get a sharp twinge in my heart when I see him coming my way or giving me that smile. And when we talk, which we still do, I have to focus a lot of energy into guarding my heart from being swept away again. Why is that? I don't even know for sure. But I do know that God is helping me through this, and I believe that He's using my weakness to make me strong—in Him. And that's not a bad thing.

HEART SMART
only You can
guard my heart
keep it safe
make me smart
help me learn
help me choose
Your way, Lord
so i don't lose
keep me honest
keep me true
let me save
my heart for You
amen

Friday, May 6

We were doing our M and S tonight when a girl about my age came up to me. She said her name was Haley and she was from Memphis. She had a tattoo of a black widow spider on her left hand and more piercings than I'll ever have, about thirty I'm guessing. Her hair was partially shaved and what remained was dyed green and blue and purple, kind of a rainbow effect. Naturally, I complimented her on her hair colors. Without even responding, she looked me straight in the eyes and asked how I could possibly know that God was for real. It was more of a challenge than a question.

So I thought about it for a moment before I said, "I used to be an atheist, Haley. I mean, I absolutely did NOT believe in God, not at all."

She looked skeptical. "Really?"

I nodded. "Yeah, I actually find it pretty hard to believe myself now. I've changed a lot since then."

"What happened?"

"Faith."

"What do you mean?"

"It's kind of hard to explain faith. First of all, no matter how badly you might want it, it's not something you can manufacture in yourself. It's a gift that God gives. Of course, I didn't understand that when I was obsessed with not believing in God. But even back then, I could see that being an atheist was definitely not working for me. I had reached this place in my life where I was totally miserable. I didn't even want to live anymore."

"So what'd you do?"

I went on to tell her about how I was so bummed about everything, and how I went to the cemetery and read the words on Clay Berringer's gravestone, a quote from Jesus that said, "I am the way and the truth and the life. No one comes to the Father except through me."

"That's the moment when God gave me the faith I needed to believe in Him," I told her. "And I know it was from God because there's no way I could've made something like that up myself."

"So you honestly believe it's real?"

"I know it's real. God is like the air I breathe," I told her. "I believe I would literally die without Him. I wonder how I ever lived before He came into my heart." I smiled at her. "I guess I didn't."

Her face was pinched up like she was trying not to cry. "I just don't know. I mean, there are these kids who say they're Christians, but they seem kind of stuck up..." She glanced toward the exit, and I wondered if she was thinking about making a break for it.

"That happens sometimes, Haley. But it's not fair to judge God based on how some ignorant people act. You need to get to know Him for who He really is, for yourself."

She seemed to be considering this.

"Do you want me to pray with you?" I asked. Now I have to admit that this is something I'm not that comfortable with, at least not by myself. I don't like to come across as too pushy. I mean, I figure if God is doing a number on someone's heart, they don't need me pressuring them too. But Allie and Laura are perfectly fine doing this, and I usually rely on them to help me out. But I glanced over my shoulder to see that they were both busy with fans. In the same instant, I noticed Jeremy nearby and he wasn't talking to anyone, but I really didn't want to ask for his help. I quickly turned back to Haley and smiled.

"I guess so," she said.

So, silently praying for God's help, I bowed my head and began to pray for her. I don't even remember what exactly I prayed for, but I felt as though I was bumbling along and probably making a mess of everything, when I felt a hand on my shoulder. I looked up to see that Jeremy had joined us and put a hand on Haley's shoulder too. When he started to pray, I actually felt my eyes filling with tears. It was so powerful and amazing. It's like he knew everything about this girl and her need for God and just everything. He even got her to pray with him, actually inviting God into her heart. Incredible! By the time he said amen, both Haley and I were crying. I gave her a big hug. "Welcome to God's family." Then I sneaked her a free CD, which I will replace from my own personal stash, and one of the tracts that Omega provides for us to give to new believers that even has a website with more helpful information.

"Your life will never be the same again," Jeremy reassured her. Then a couple of other kids came up and joined her. It turned out they were her cousins, kids who'd been witnessing to her for years. Haley and I hugged again, and I told her that I'd be praying for her, and then they left.

"Thanks, Jeremy," I said, feeling a little self-conscious. "I was kind of floundering there."

"Hey, you were willing. That's what counts."

"But how did you know I needed help?"

"I guess it was a God-thing." He smiled.

I nodded, at the same time telling myself to watch my heart—no major meltdowns for me tonight. "Well, I appreciate it." I waved over to Allie.

Now the most miraculous part of this evening was the simple way God pulled Haley right into His arms. I know it was the result of His perfect timing and everything, but it was amazing to participate in, amazing to witness.

But in a smaller way, I was amazed at how I kept my heart under control. Despite the impressive way Jeremy prayed and ministered to Haley—which would've normally attracted me like a magnet—I managed to maintain that safe distance. I managed to keep myself from plunging into the depths of infatuation and experiencing another full-blown crush. I've decided that a crush is exactly what it sounds like—it can crush your heart. In other words, not good. At least not for me. For me, a crush is to be avoided at all costs. What a relief it is to know this.

AGAIN AND AGAIN
You've done it again
amazing God
drawing our hearts to You
again and again
You pull us toward You
like flowers to the sun
like the waves to the shore
like rain to the earth
again and again
You pull us toward You
our hearts merge with Yours
and we become one
with You
again and again
amen

Eight

Saturday, May 14

Today has been nothing but pure fun from the very get-go, and it's not even time for the prom yet. First Allie and Laura and I met Beanie at the Paradiso (the local coffeehouse). And it's always pretty cool to be back in the very first place I ever performed. But to our pleased surprise, Caitlin was there too. (Not even Josh knew that she was coming home this weekend.)

Anyway, it was so amazing to just sit there with Beanie and Caitlin and to consider what a profound influence these two college girls have had on our lives. I took a moment to just study them, and I thought to myself, man, these girls are as different as night and day. Okay, that might be too extreme since they both totally love God. But where Caitlin is this very thoughtful and sometimes reserved blue-eyed blonde, Beanie is a dark-eyed brunette who has this huge snorting laugh that makes everyone turn and look. But they're both beautiful women, and I am truly glad they're our friends.

So there we all sat just laughing and talking and enjoying this incredible reunion while consuming way too much caffeine until it was nearly noon. After that, we headed over to my house to try out our prom outfits with Beanie's supervision and final tweaking. Well, that girl really outdid herself this time.

I must confess I was concerned about this whole fifties thing, imagining us wearing puffy pastel dresses that looked like they'd survived a bad wedding party, but I'm willing to admit when I'm wrong.

"It's because of Chloe that I chose the fifties," announced Beanie as she laid out the garment bags containing our outfits.

"What do you mean?" I asked, instantly on the defense.

"I wanted to see you wearing something a little more feminine for a change," said Beanie. "Your Doc Martens are fine and everything, but I thought it'd be fun to see you really looking like a girly girl."

Naturally, Laura and Allie got a good laugh over this since they both think I'm not terribly in touch with my feminine side. Which I happen to think is a bunch of bunk. I mean, just because you don't wear lace and frills doesn't mean you're not feminine. Right?

But what can you do when you're outnumbered— four to one in this case since Caitlin had come along to see our little dress rehearsal? And God bless Caitlin because she said, "Chloe is very feminine. Who else can dress like she does and still look that pretty?" Okay, "pretty" probably isn't the look I'm usually going for, but it was better than nothing.

Now let me describe our outfits in the order that Beanie presented them to us. First was Allie's, a pretty little chiffon number in a soft shade of aqua blue that really brought out her blue eyes. But instead of being all fluffy and poofy, it was more sleek and sophisticated.

"I feel like a real movie star." Allie twirled around in it, pointing the toe of a satin dyed-to-match strappy shoe. "Very sexy."

"Yeah," said Laura. "Reminds me of Marilyn Monroe."

"Wait 'til you see the rhinestones I have to go with it." Beanie dug through a bag to produce a necklace, earrings, and bracelet that looked surprisingly like the real thing—diamonds.

"You should let me help you with your hair," offered Caitlin. "You'll want to wear it up."

"Cool." Allie grinned as she scooped her blond waves into a makeshift do and strutted around my bedroom. But then she started singing "Diamonds are a Girl's Best Friend" until we finally had to shut her up.

Next came Laura. It figured that Beanie was making me (queen of the heel draggers) wait until last. Laura's outfit, in my opinion, was even more stunning than Allie's. It was this amazing shade of orangeish coral, but in an iridescent satin that just seemed to shimmer with all kinds of hidden colors, and believe me, it looked totally amazing against Laura's beautiful bronze-colored skin. The dress wasn't as soft looking as Allie's. In fact, as I search for the right word to describe it, I think I would call it smoldering. I could imagine Laura in a smoky nightclub crooning out the blues. Okay, I realize Laura would never do that—I'm simply being dramatic. And the satin shoes to go with it were absolutely gorgeous, sleek and simple, yet very elegant.

"Ooh," Laura said as she checked herself out in the mirror. "This is nice. Very nice."

"Poor Ryan," said Allie. "He's going to fall over dead when he sees you looking so hot."

Laura laughed. "Good. Then at least he'll have something to remember me by."

Naturally, we were all curious as to what this meant, but Laura quickly set us straight.

"I've decided that going to the prom with Ryan is going to be just a one-date thing," she explained as Beanie helped her with the necklace clasp (a beautiful string of oversize faux black pearls and earrings to match).

Laura turned to me. "Can we tell them about our pact?"

"Fine with me," I said and Allie nodded. And then the three of us attempted to explain our commitment. It came out in something of a jumble, but Caitlin and Beanie seemed to get it.

And Caitlin—no surprise here—thought it was a very wise plan. "Take it from me, you'll all save yourself a whole lot of trouble," she said. "And I know that God will honor you for it. Just wait and see."

Beanie nodded, mumbling with pins in her mouth as she took in the back of Laura's dress. "She's right, you know. I should've listened to Caitlin when I was your age."

Finally, it was my turn. And Beanie's psychology was working on me. I couldn't wait. By now I figured that even if she pulled out a powder pink dress that looked like something from "Beauty and the Beast," I'd still be happy. After all, she's Beanie and she just has ways of making things look good. But I was totally delighted when she unzipped the garment bag to reveal a burgundy-colored dress in a silky fabric that felt as soft as butter. "It's beautiful," I told her as she helped me slip into it.

"Don't you feel like royalty?"

I nodded. "I love the way the skirt feels around my legs."

"That little slit makes it great for dancing too," she said as she zipped up the little zipper beneath my arm.

The fitted bodice had lots of tucks that gave it its shape, and I'm guessing it would probably have worked perfectly fine as a strapless dress, but just the same, I felt thankful for the sleek spaghetti straps.

"You look stunning," said Caitlin. "I mean it, Chloe, you are hot!"

Everyone seemed to agree, and I wasn't sure if it was all just part of an elaborate plan to get me to comply with this whole dressing up thing, but hey, I was already on board. This was turning out to be a lot more fun than I'd expected.

"These shoes are actually from the fifties." Beanie produced a gorgeous pair of black velvet high heels with dainty little ankle straps. "They're just like new. Not cheap either, but I think they're worth it, don't you?"

"I love them," I said as I slipped them on.

Then she brought out another set of jewelry. "Okay. I have to warn you that, like the shoes, these are the real thing too. They're actually from the forties. They're gold plated and the stones are garnets, and considering their value, I got a real deal on them. Still, they were kind of spendy compared to the other pieces, and if you think they're too much, the lady at the second-hand shop promised I can return them."

But as soon as I had them on, everyone insisted that I had to keep them. And I had no problem with that. I liked the idea of wearing something from another era. It's like those sparkling red stones could have a story to tell. That's pretty cool.

"Beanie," said Caitlin. "Doesn't this remind you of the time that you, Jenny, and I went to the prom? Only minus the guys."

"Except no way were our threads as cool as these."

"Yeah," said Caitlin. "We couldn't have afforded it."

Allie sighed. "It wasn't that long ago that I never would've been able to afford it either. Sometimes I think I'm just having a really good dream."

So I pinched her, gently. "It's for real."

Then we wrote out the check that Willy had given us to pay Beanie for the clothes and her valuable time.

"Willy made us promise that we'd wear these outfits during a concert sometime," I explained. "That way they're deductible."

"Sounds good to me," Laura said as she admired herself in the mirror one last time before Beanie made her take off the dress.

"I'll do the final alterations and have them

back to you girls by six. Is that early enough?"

"Perfect," I told her. "We'll be here."

Then I went for a bike ride, read my Bible, took a short nap, and still had time to write all this down in my diary. But now it's almost six, and I'm guessing everyone will be here soon. My first prom and I feel like just a regular high school girl again (or maybe for the first time). Basically, I can't wait!

WITH ABANDON
fill me, Lord
with joy so sweet
that i dance
with happy feet
let my life
ring clear and true
reflecting what
i see in You
with arms outstretched
and reaching high
hear me rejoice
right through the sky
with sweet abandon
i will sing
and worship You
my only King
amen

Nine

Sunday, May 15

Last night (prom night) was full of surprises. Where to start? Why not just begin at the beginning.

Beanie and Caitlin helped us to get ready (hair and makeup and the works). Man, from all the excitement going on around here you'd have thought we were doing a major concert or maybe attending the music awards to pick up our Grammy. But it was fun having both Caitlin and Beanie helping us. Afterward, Allie jokingly suggested that we bring them both on tour with us sometime, and I have to say that Caitlin and Beanie both acted pretty interested.

Anyway, the plan was for the guys to come over here early so that Beanie could get some photos of the six of us (her final project) with her teacher's fancy digital camera. Isaiah and Brett were staying at a hotel downtown, and Ryan, of course, was at his parents'. We expected them to get here around seven, then following our photo session, we would all climb into my VW van and ride to the big event together. My dad had even washed and cleaned it out inside—very sweet of him.

To say my parents (mostly my mom) were totally excited is an understatement. My mom seemed almost like she was a teenager herself as we got ready, she was so into it. And I didn't even mind having her hang with us. It was really fun having her involved and seeing her so happy. Okay, it was more than fun, it was unforgettably cool.

So we were all dolled up and Ryan was already here, and I must say he looked fantastic in his fifties-style suit, black with pinstripes, but he looked pretty nervous too. Laura said it was only because he was excited about meeting "two of the guys from Iron Cross." Well, whatever. Like our agreement, we three girls aren't letting any guys mess us up.

But then I almost lost it when I saw the other guys coming up the walk to my house. I'll admit that Isaiah and Brett looked amazing in their suits, but what just about undid me was the fact that Jeremy was WITH them. Now, I didn't get that. What was he doing here?

Turned out he'd come along just to hang with them in our little town for a couple of days and, as he said, "to absorb some of the local flavor." Well. And he'd driven the guys over in their rental car so he could use it while we we're out "promming." Well again.

Now you'd think he'd have left after dropping the young men off, but no, he decided to stick around and watch the photo session. Did he hang around just to impress Beanie and Caitlin, who acted like a couple of overgrown groupies, getting everyone's autographs as they took photos of all three guys? Or was it something else? Okay, before it sounds as though I'm getting carried away here (and I have NOT forgotten our pact), I have to say that he was paying me some very specific attention.

"You look different, Chloe. It's like you're all grown up now."

I frowned at him. "It's just an outfit, Jeremy."

"I know, but it really makes you seem older."

Then Isaiah came up and hooked my arm in his. "Keep your hands off my woman, bro."

We all laughed, but the look in Jeremy's eyes (I don't think I imagined this) seemed almost hurt. Now, I know this makes absolutely no sense. I'm only writing it down because it was so weird—and surprising—and slightly confusing.

Caitlin even pulled me aside before we left. "Chloe, does Jeremy like you?"

I shrugged. "We're all friends. We hang out together a lot, you know?"

"I know. But Chloe, does he _like_ you?"

Now, if there was ever a chick I felt I could be totally honest with (the girl reads me like a book) it is Caitlin. And so I told her, "He has a girlfriend, Caitlin, but I am just getting over a very serious crush on him. We're like brother and sister, you know? Does that answer your question?"

She nodded. "Sort of. But listen, Chloe, that look on his face looked like something more than just brother and sister."

Well, I could feel my cheeks starting to flush then, and I just wished that Caitlin hadn't said a thing. And yet, at the same time, I was thrilled that she did. Why is that? But as a result I did something that was probably very stupid and immature (but hey, I'm only seventeen). I started cozying up to Isaiah and acting all silly, like I honestly thought he'd hung the moon or something. I can't even explain it without making myself sound totally moronic.

It wasn't long after my little stunt that Jeremy left, and then I really felt bad. But I reminded myself that: 1) Jeremy has a girlfriend, 2) he's too old for me, and 3) Isaiah and I were just out to have a good time and a few laughs tonight. Basically, I told myself to just chill and have fun. And fortunately we did.

I was really glad that we didn't hire a limo like Allie had suggested. We already felt like we had celebrity status anyway once we stepped into the ballroom—we were running late since we took our time over the swankiest dinner our town has to offer.

But thanks to Tiffany Knight, the word had gotten around that two guys from "another rock band" were escorting Allie and me. And even though not all the kids at school listen to, or even know of, Iron Cross, they all acted pretty interested in getting a glimpse of Isaiah and Brett. Fortunately, it didn't take long for everyone to get their looks and then get back to the normal business of visiting and dancing, and before long we were all just part of the big noisy crowd.

Another happy surprise of the evening was that Cesar (yes, I've-kissed-dating-goodbye Cesar) was there. He was with Marty Ruez.

"It's not a real date," Marty informed me. "Cesar's just being nice because he knew that no one else would ask me."

"I just figured there was no reason the two of us couldn't hang out together and have a good time without calling it date," said Cesar.

I felt like hugging him just then. Good old Cesar. What a guy. I proudly introduced him to Isaiah, saying, "Cesar and I used to date, but now he's given up dating altogether."

Isaiah frowned. "Man, I hope it wasn't anything personal, Chloe."

I acted as if I were mad, then quickly told Cesar that Isaiah and I weren't dating either. "We're just friends," I said, worried that Cesar might get the wrong impression. I'm not even sure

why this bothered me, but for some reason I
didn't want to do anything to hurt Cesar
tonight—or ever for that matter. I think Cesar
will always have a special place in my heart.
And if not for the whole stupid thing with
Jeremy, I'd probably still have feelings for
Cesar. Isn't life funny?

"Hey, speak for yourself," said Isaiah. "For all
we know, I could be falling in love tonight."

But I knew he was just joking.

Just then Tiffany came back over. She'd been
dogging our heels since we'd arrived. "I wanted
you and Isaiah to meet my date," she told me as
she shoved a tall blond guy toward me, blocking
Marty and Cesar. "This is Adam Brown. You
probably don't know him since he goes to
McFadden. I met him at youth group."

Adam smiled, but I could tell he was uncomfortable. "I've heard a lot of good things about
you, Chloe." Then he looked at Isaiah in a
slightly starstruck way. "And I have an Iron
Cross CD. Uh, it's really good."

"Thanks," said Isaiah.

Then trying to be polite, since Tiffany seemed
clueless, I introduced Adam to Cesar and Marty,
who were still standing nearby.

"They're not really dating," said Tiffany, as if
it mattered.

"Well, we're not really dating either," I told her, winking at Isaiah.

Tiffany studied Marty carefully, and fearing Tiffany was about to let loose with a cutting remark, I decided to head her off at the pass.

"You look absolutely great," I said to Marty. "That dark blue is striking on you. Really brings out your eyes."

"The lady at the mall told me it was slimming."

I heard Tiffany clear her throat.

"She must be right," I said quickly. "Or else you've lost weight."

Marty smiled. "Thanks, Chloe. You're not looking too bad yourself. I hardly recognized you tonight."

I laughed. "Yeah, everyone keeps saying that. I guess no one really thought I knew how to dress like a girl."

"Where did you get that dress?" said Tiffany. Thankfully she was distracted from Marty now.

"Beanie Jacobs designed our outfits," I told her. Not that it would mean anything to her since Beanie had graduated before Tiffany and I ever started high school.

"Oh yeah, I think I saw some of her stuff in 'Vogue' recently."

I maintained my poker face as I nodded, then reminded myself to let Beanie know that her career has launched much faster than anyone imagined possible.

Another surprise of the evening was that Marissa had come with Jake. "Just as friends," she quickly assured me. "It was Cesar's idea. We doubled with him and Marty. I tried to bribe Marty into trading dates with me, but naturally she refused. At least we got to come in the same car together."

"So you're still chasing after poor Cesar?"

Marissa stood up straighter, adjusting the top of her black strapless dress, which in my opinion exposed more cleavage than necessary. I'm guessing this was intended more for Cesar than Jake.

"Hey, he can't give up women forever."

I started to say that it was more than that, but I realized she'd probably already heard this dozens of times. Sometimes people just believe what they want to believe.

Well, our group of six really worked that prom. We mixed it up with just about everyone, which I must say was rather cool. Another big surprise of the evening was when Jessie Oldfield (my old best friend from middle school, before I turned into a rebel) came over to talk to me. I didn't even know that she'd moved back.

"You look great, Chloe."

"Thanks, Jess. So do you."

"Hey, I've been meaning to write you or something." Jessie looked down, fiddling with her wrist corsage. "I know I wasn't very nice to you in middle school, and I just wanted to say that I'm sorry."

I put my hand on her shoulder. "No problem. Really. I just needed to go through some hard stuff back then. But ultimately it led me to God, and that's what truly matters."

"I know."

I blinked. "Really? You know about God?"

She nodded. "And it has a lot to do with what you're doing. I got your CD, which I think is awesome by the way, and I listened to it over and over, and I read all the lyrics and really thought about what it all meant. I guess it just started making me hungry for God too. I asked Jesus into my heart a couple of months ago."

"That is so cool, Jessie!"

"Yeah." She smiled. "It is, isn't it? Anyway, I hope we can be friends again, but I wouldn't blame you if you—"

"Hey, if you're a Christian you should know about forgiveness by now."

"I do. But I also know that you can't force other people to forgive you."

"Well, I totally forgive you, Jess. I did that a long time ago."

We talked some more and agreed to stay in

touch through e-mail. Now that was something I never would've expected to happen—ever. So to say this day was full of surprises is absolutely the truth.

SURPRISES
unexpected
unsuspected
life with God
is a wild ride
it's exciting
and delighting
when you're standing
on His side
it's worth living
and forgiving
what's the risk
so take a chance
on believing
and receiving
love and joy
begin the dance
cm

Ten

Tuesday, May 17

We have two more concerts (Friday and Saturday), both with Iron Cross, but after that we come back home for the two weeks of school preceding graduation. Then Laura can participate in all her senior activities that Mrs. Mitchell feels are so important. This was agreed upon before we went back on tour this spring. At the time I felt a little resentful, but after going to the prom on Saturday, I understand better how these times really are important. And I wouldn't want to take that away from Laura.

Speaking of Laura, she did "break it off" with Ryan. Not that they were exactly going together, but Laura said that he seemed pretty surprised and slightly hurt when she told him she didn't have the time or energy to have a boyfriend in her life right now.

"It was weird," she told us the next day. "I mean, I didn't really think Ryan was all that interested in me since James had said how Ryan was all bummed about this other girl. But when he realized that I wasn't interested, well, it was like he was really interested in me and practically begged me to reconsider."

Allie laughed. "Now, what is up with that?"

"Maybe it's the old hard-to-get routine," I suggested. "You act like you're all uninterested, and suddenly the guy is totally nuts for you."

"Too bad more girls don't understand this concept," said Allie.

"Or not," I said.

"What about guys?" asked Laura. "Don't they play hard to get?"

"Yeah, and I think guys are better at it than girls," I said. "Think about it. They don't usually throw their hearts down onto the table for everyone to look at. Not the way girls do anyway."

"Maybe that's why the girls are usually chasing the guys," said Allie.

And I do think we're onto something. I mean, I'm trying not to think about the way Jeremy acted on prom night. At first I thought I was imagining it, but then Caitlin noticed it too. And so there's this little part of me that thinks Jeremy may have gotten just the teensiest bit interested in me because he saw me going out with his brother. Now that's all I'm going to say about that because I want to honor my pact with Laura and Allie, and I do not want to start falling all over myself in love with Jeremy Baxter again. Phew.

                    SURRENDER
                 my heart is Yours
                 it's in Your hand
                 my life is Yours
                i'll make my stand
                 all i am, Lord
                  all i will be
                  i give to You
                like You give to me
                  i lay it down
                 before Your feet
                  i give my all
                 Lord, it is sweet
                  to trust in You
                 to live in grace
                 to know Your love
                  to see Your face
                     amen

Sunday, May 22

Our concerts both went fine this week. Without a
hitch, as Willy would say, although I thought
they lacked a little something in energy. It was
hard to tell whether it was due to the musicians
or the crowd. But I must say that even Iron Cross
didn't seem as hot as usual. Maybe it was just
something in the air.

But now we're on our way home again (only four hours away). And we three girls are all very glad. I think we're a little worn out. A couple of weeks at home sounds like just the break we need. But now let me write down the most exciting thing to happen this week. In fact, I would call it <u>breaking news!</u>

Without letting on to any of us girls, Willy proposed to Elise last night and she has accepted. We were all pretty shocked when they told us today. Talk about your clandestine romance. I mean, we sort of knew that Willy had it bad for Elise. But none of us, not even Allie, had the slightest inclination that Elise felt the same way about him. That woman should get an Oscar for her performance.

"How did you keep it to yourselves this whole time?" demanded Allie at breakfast this morning, after the happy couple shared the news. Allie wasn't really mad about the engagement but simply irritated that she hadn't seen it coming better.

"I was only trying to set a good example for you girls," Elise explained. "I thought maybe, since I'm supposed to be the chaperone, well, it was better if you didn't see Willy and me acting all mushy and goofy."

Willy grinned. "We'll be saving that for later."

Elise winked at him. "But there is a little problem now."

"I called Eric Green this morning," said Willy. "I explained our situation and expressed our concern about having Redemption's chaperone be engaged to the manager while we're on tour. I know it probably sounds a little old-fashioned on my part, but I was concerned about how it might appear to the public, you know?"

"I don't see anything wrong with it," said Allie.

"I don't know," said Laura. "I don't mean to be a wet blanket here, but I can't help wondering what my mom would say about the whole thing. You know how she can be."

"And she's not totally wrong," said Willy. "If we err here, I would rather we err on the side of prudence. You know a lot of people are watching Redemption and following your every move. We don't want to do anything with the least bit of impropriety that might harm your reputation."

"But who will we get for our chaperone?" Allie glanced over to where Rosy was at the counter refilling her coffee cup. "Hey, maybe Rosy can do it."

"She could, and we all know she's a great help. But she needs to focus her attention on the driving end of things," said Willy. "That in itself is a pretty big responsibility."

"I have an idea," I said suddenly. "It was something we'd joked about a while back, but now that this has happened, well, who knows? Maybe this could be a real God-thing."

"What is it?" asked Elise as she helped Davie open his milk carton.

"What about having Caitlin O'Conner for a chaperone?"

Willy nodded. "You know, that's not a bad idea. Do you think she'd be interested?"

"Yes! Yes!" shrieked Allie. "That is totally perfect."

"And how about Beanie too?" asked Laura eagerly. "She could be our wardrobe designer on the road."

"I think you girls may be onto something," said Willy.

"Caitlin and Beanie will both be done with school by the time we leave for tour again," I said. "The timing is perfect."

"What about in the fall?" asked Elise. "When it's time for Caitlin and Beanie to return to school?"

"I'm not sure," I said. "But remember, Jesus said we only need to worry about one day at a time."

"God will take care of the rest," said Allie happily.

So we e-mailed Caitlin and Beanie right after breakfast. And Willy discussed it with Eric Green. And by the end of the day, it was settled.

Not only would we have Caitlin as chaperone, but we'd have Beanie as wardrobe designer. Both on salary.

Man, this is so totally cool. Not that we don't love Elise—we definitely do. And she's been a great chaperone. But having Caitlin and Beanie will be so awesome. And as far as keeping us in line (like we're such a problem—okay, maybe sometimes), I have no doubt whatsoever that the level-headed Caitlin O'Conner will have no trouble keeping us on track. Not only that, but she said in her e-mail that she has a new devotional book that she wants to take us through during our summer tour. This is going to be so cool!

MY PSALM OF PRAISE
Your plans are greater than the seas
Your ways are higher than the mountains
Your thoughts are vaster than the deserts
Your mercy is wider than the sky
Your joy is deeper than the ocean
Your love is bigger than the universe
Awesome God, You are mighty!
amen

Eleven

Wednesday, May 25

If you have to be in school, and I'm not complaining because there are definitely some things that I miss, you might do it during the last two weeks of the school year. I suppose there's not a lot of quality schoolwork going on this time of year, but everyone seems to be in a happy mood and the social life is great. Of course, I didn't think this way a couple of years ago. Man, how life can change when you let God into it. I was reminded of this in a major way when I got a note from Mrs. King (school counselor) this afternoon.

Now the last time I got a note from Mrs. King was when I was in deep doo-doo for smacking Kerry Fraley in the face with my backpack and consequently breaking her nose. Okay, it was self-defense, but at the same time it was getting ugly with criminal charges threatening to be pressed and whatnot. Anyway, that all flashed back on me as I walked to her office. Of course, I knew that I wasn't really in trouble today. I mean, I've done nothing wrong. But just the same it felt pretty weird, and I even experienced a serious wave of guilt as I walked into her office.

"Hi, Chloe," she said with a bright smile. "Long time no see."

"Yeah, it's been a crazy year."

"Have a seat."

I sat down, still trying to repress these misplaced feelings of guilt. "What's up?"

"Well, I've been talking to some of your teachers..."

I frowned. "But my grades have been okay. What's wrong?"

"Nothing's wrong, Chloe." She tapped her fingers on her desk as if she was thinking. "And I'm not even sure that I should suggest this, but I think I would be wrong not to at least mention it."

"What?"

"Well, your grades are great, Chloe, but more than that, your teachers feel your work is far above your grade level. Some of your papers would have earned A's at college level."

"Really?" Now I was stunned.

"Really. In fact, that's why you're here. I wouldn't normally suggest this to a student, but you're an exception. Since your band is doing so well and you seem to have your life going down this amazing track that other kids only dream of, I'd like to recommend that you graduate early, Chloe. But I fully realize this is your decision and you may not even want to."

"How?" I asked eagerly. "How can I do that?"

"Oh, it's not too difficult. You'll have to take certain classes in the fall, and there are some tests to take. But I'm sure you'll have no problem with it. That is, if you choose to do this. And it's up to you, and your parents, of course."

"I'd like to think about it." I paused. "And I need to pray about it and talk to my parents and stuff."

"I have a letter here." She held up an official-looking envelope. "There's a permission slip for your parents and some other things. You don't have to make up your mind until fall."

"Thanks." I grinned at her. "You know, when I was walking to the office I was thinking about how I got into so much trouble during my fresh-man year. Do you remember?"

She laughed. "Yeah. You were something else. But I could tell, even then, that you had some-thing pretty special going on."

"Really?"

She nodded. "You're quite a girl, Chloe."

"Thanks. But I have to give the credit to God. Without Him, I am a complete mess."

She smiled. "I figured you'd say something like that. Well, keep up the good work and good luck with your band. My thirteen-year-old loves your CD, and she's even taken up the guitar in hopes that she can grow up to be like you. In fact..." Mrs. King looked slightly embarrassed

now. "She'd love it if I brought home your autograph. Do you mind?"

I laughed. "Not at all." And so I signed a piece
of notepaper "To Becky, with love, Chloe Miller."

"Thanks. I'll be her hero tonight."

I told my parents about Mrs. King's idea as we
were cleaning up the kitchen after dinner. And
for some reason I thought my mom was going to
balk. Maybe it was a flashback to the old days or
perhaps it's because Laura's mom has reacted to
so many things in an overprotective way. But my
mom totally surprised me by saying that she felt
it was my decision and was completely comfortable with whatever I chose.

"I'm with your mom," agreed Dad as he hung up
the dish towel. "And I'm not even surprised that
they're offering this to you, Chloe. We've always
known you were a smart girl."

"Sometimes you were too smart for your own
good," Mom said with a sly smile. "But it looks
like you've grown into it. By the way, honey, have
I told you that I'm really proud of you?"

I had to laugh because that's becoming one of
her favorite lines of late. But then I'm not tired of
hearing it either. In fact, coming from her, it means
more than almost anything to me. I can't believe
how much she's changed since she and Dad started
going to church regularly. Anyway, I hugged her
and told her I loved her, and we both got a little

teary eyed. I'm not even sure why we cried exactly.
I guess it was over all the things we've been
through in the past, all the times I thought she
hated me or was embarrassed by me or just didn't
care. Now I know I was wrong. Thank God.

GROWING
growing up
and growing old
learn to do
the things we're told
growing up
and growing wise
learn to see through
others' eyes
growing up
and growing fast
hope the good times
don't zip past
growing up
and growing smart
i know i won't
outgrow God's heart
cm

Friday, May 27
I reintroduced myself to an old friend today. I'm
sure she thought that I'd completely forgotten

her. But I didn't. Okay, here is what I remember about Kim Peterson. When I was in eighth grade and going through my little rebellious streak, and consequently losing my old friends left and right, I was on my way to orchestra one day (believe it or not, I used to play the violin—and not all that well) when Kim spoke to me.

"You know, you could be a much better musician if you took the violin more seriously," she said as we reached the door.

"Huh?" I stopped and looked at her as if she were an alien.

"I know you probably think I'm a geek because I actually care about school and grades and orchestra and all that."

"Aren't you that brainy chick who has some big record for winning the mental math contest for like about twenty consecutive years?"

"Four, actually."

"Yeah, whatever."

"But, really, Chloe, I've watched you play violin and you're good, but you just don't take it seriously. I'll bet you never even practice."

I nodded. "You got that right."

"And I know that you're having a hard time this year..."

Now this made me mad. I didn't need little Miss Perfect telling me how to live my life right then. "It's none of your business," I snapped at her.

"Fine." She held her head up high, and I could tell that I'd offended her, but I still didn't care. "I just wanted to let you know that I think you could be a good musician if you worked harder."

And believe it or not, those words of hers stuck with me. But instead of practicing my violin (and honestly I never thought I'd have a chance of bumping her out of first chair because I was certain that she practiced for at least six hours each day), I decided to take up the guitar. And thinking about what she'd said about music, I decided to take my guitar seriously, and I actually began practicing for several hours a day too. Of course, I never told her any of this back then. But in some ways, I've always felt that Kim Peterson had a little to do with my success in music.

Anyway, when I saw her heading in the direction of the music department, I called out to her and she stopped.

"Hey, Kim, do you remember me?"

She kind of rolled her eyes like she thought I was a half-wit. "Yes, Chloe, everyone in town knows who you are. The famous leader of the Christian rock band Redemption."

"Yeah, whatever. So, how are you doing?"

"Okay, I guess. Are you actually enrolled in school now or just popping in to sign autographs?"

I had to laugh at her attitude. It was obvious that this chick wasn't anything like some of the other kids who practically grovel and bow, acting as if I should rule the world just because I have a recording contract.

"I'm here until the end of the school year," I told her. "Mostly so that Laura Mitchell can graduate with her class."

"Lucky Laura." Her voice sound exasperated as she pushed a black strand of silky hair from her eyes. Then she just stood there for a moment and studied me, with what seemed a very calculated interest, before she started walking toward the music department again. And although uninvited, I walked along with her. Finally, we were just outside the orchestra room, but I still wasn't sure what I wanted to say.

"Looks like you're still playing violin," I said as I nodded down to her well-worn leather case.

"Yeah, unlike you, I haven't had any great offers to start leading a rock band yet."

I shrugged. "Hey, as I recall you were pretty good on your violin."

She almost smiled now.

"In fact," I said suddenly remembering something. "There's a song I've been working on that I really think needs a violin backup. Do you have any interest in jamming with us this weekend?"

"Jamming?"

"You know, just playing for fun. To see how it sounds."

She seemed to consider this. "Maybe."

"Well, we practice for most of the day on Saturday. Give me a call if you're interested."

She nodded and started to go into the orchestra room.

"And Kim," I called out.

She turned and looked at me with an expression that was a mixture of irritation and curiosity.

"I just wanted to apologize for that time, back in middle school, when I acted like a jerk when you were trying to encourage me about music."

Now she gave me the blankest expression, as if she didn't even remember the incident, and maybe she didn't. Then she just shrugged. "Yeah, whatever." She turned and went into orchestra.

Now, if I hadn't known Kim (or at least observed her) for a number of years, I might've actually thought she was being a total snob just then. But I really think that she purposely keeps to herself sometimes, probably as a protective device. Especially with people she doesn't know or trust that well. Like me. I think it's partially because she's Asian (Korean, as I recall) and because she's adopted. But I could be imagining all this. It may be that her greatest challenge in life is the fact that she's just really, really smart. So much so that she has been teased mercilessly over the years.

In fact, she and I used to be in the TAG program together (Talented and Gifted). But it wasn't long before I realized that being in TAG was like wearing a great big target that said "pick on me, I'm smart," and so, to much parental displeasure, I dropped out. Poor Kim didn't figure this out, or maybe her parents wouldn't let her quit, but she remained in TAG and consequently suffered the abuse that comes with membership.

Now, as senseless as this may sound, I feel somewhat responsible for her abuse all these years later. Don't even ask me why. It's not that I ever did much more than shut her down that day she tried to encourage me. But I do regret it. And maybe it's a God-thing, but I do hope that she'll join us to jam on Saturday. And I wasn't making that up. I really have been wondering what some string backup would sound like with this new song I'm working on.

No, I'm not going to invite her to join Redemption as the fourth member of our band. I think we sound just right as we are. But I may invite her to be my friend. If she's interested, that is.

PRAYER FOR KIM
i see the sadness in her eyes
i wonder, does she realize
how much You love, how much You care
does she know, would she dare
could she give her heart to You
live for You her whole life through?
touch her, Jesus, with Your love
with Your mercy from above
show her there's a better way
turn her nighttime into day
amen

Twelve

Saturday, May 28

Much to our surprise, Kim Peterson did show up to jam with us today. And after a while, she really loosened up and showed us her stuff.

"Man," said Allie. "You are really good, Kim."

She smiled. "Thanks."

"It makes me wish that more of our songs would work with a violin," I said.

Kim laughed now. "Nah, you guys have a great sound already. Sometimes when I listen to your CD, I almost forget that it's Christian music."

I frowned. "Really?"

"Hey, I mean it as a compliment. The truth is you won't catch me listening to much Christian music. Mostly it's too preachy and weird. It kind of gives me the heebie-jeebies."

"If you don't listen to it, how do you know that?" asked Laura.

"My mom listens to it all the time," said Kim as she put her violin back in its case. "Ugh. I get so sick of it."

I nodded. "Well, maybe she listens to the wrong kind of music. Maybe if she heard Iron Cross or—"

"No way," said Kim. "My mom is definitely not into any kind of rock whatsoever, Christian or otherwise."

"So, do you plan to do anything with your music?" I asked as she closed up her case.

She shrugged. "I don't know. Mr. Covell, in orchestra, says I could probably get a music scholarship. But my parents don't think a profession in music offers much financial stability for my future."

Laura laughed. "Tell us about it. You should've heard my mom before we signed our contract with Omega."

"My mom was just as bad," I offered. "But they've started to sing a different tune."

"Yeah," said Kim. "But what happened to you guys is kind of like winning the lottery. Most musicians spend their whole lives without even a tiny bit of the success that you're having." Then she smiled. "And now I can say I jammed with you."

"And if we ever need a good violinist," I told her as we walked her to the front door, "we'll know just who to call."

"I won't be holding my breath." But she smiled again and I felt that perhaps we'd made it through some kind of barrier with her.

I closed the door, then turned to Allie and Laura. "For some reason God has really put Kim on my heart. I plan to be praying for her a lot."

"She's a cool girl," said Allie. "I guess I just never took the time to get to know her before."

"She hasn't been the easiest person to get to know," said Laura. "I think she's got a couple of close friends, but she pretty much holds everyone off at arm's length."

"Probably because she's afraid," I said.

"Of what?"

"You know, of getting hurt. I even hurt her myself one time, back in middle school."

"Are you saying that she could be more easily hurt because she's Asian?" asked Laura, her dark eyes challenging me.

"Well, what do you think? I mean, I know you're a minority at school, but at least there are quite a few African-American kids, and you've never had a problem making friends."

"Yeah," added Allie. "In fact, you weren't exactly friendly to us when we first tried to become friends with you."

"That's right," I reminded her. "And there aren't that many Asian kids at our school. Kim's in a lot more of a minority than you, Laura."

She nodded. "Okay, you might be right, at least about our school, but I'm not so sure about the bigger picture. I think Asians, in general, face less discrimination than African-Americans.

Maybe even less than Hispanics."

"Yeah," I said. "I might have to agree with you there. Although I'm not much of an expert."

"Well, if you want to hear an expert opinion, you should get my dad going sometime," said Laura.

"Okay, okay," said Allie with her typical impatience. "If we've resolved the racial questions of the day, do you think we could possibly go finish up our practice now? I promised Mom I'd watch Davie while she and Willy go out tonight."

"So, how are the lovebirds?" asked Laura.

"Talk about mush," said Allie. "They weren't kidding that they were saving it until after our tour." Then she laughed. "But it's really kind of cute. And do you know what? Mom said that rather than having Willy spend all that money on an engagement ring for her, she'd rather have him get his front tooth capped."

We all laughed about that.

"But I like Willy's gold tooth," I said. "I'm not sure if he'll still be Willy with it all fixed and pretty."

"Well apparently Willy wants it capped too," said Allie as she sat down at the drums. "See, that's what being in love can do."

"Here's to love," I said, then started our next song.

HERE'S TO LOVE
when it is right
you'll understand
that it is from
the Master's hand
when it is right
your heart will know
it's time to love
it's time to go
when it is right
you'll feel the peace
your heart will soar
with great release
when it is right
sent from above
you will rejoice
here's to love!
cm

Monday, May 30

Our church had a Memorial Day picnic at the lake today. Pastor Tony invited everyone to take a few minutes to remember friends and loved ones who are no longer here on earth. I think a lot of people were thinking about his brother Clay who was killed a few years ago in that terrible shooting at McFadden High. I know I was thinking about him. I'm still amazed at the influence his life had over me. And I never even met him. I couldn't help but think that God is amazing.

Josh had come home from college. He graduates next week. I can't believe that's possible, but he assures me it is. And if I think about it, I have to admit that my brother, who used to be an obnoxious, fairly self-absorbed preppy, has really grown up into a very nice man. I even took a moment to tell him so.

He grinned. "Thanks, Chloe. You might not know it, but that means a lot coming from you."

"Yeah," I said sarcastically. "I'm sure the opinion of your kid sister is pretty significant."

He got slightly serious then. "Hey, I have a lot of respect for you. Probably more than you can imagine without getting an even bigger head."

Then we started teasing and messing with each other just like the old days. Pretty cool. I noticed him glancing out of the corner of his eye from time to time to see where Caitlin was and who she was visiting with, since she'd come home too. Finally, I couldn't stand it.

"Josh, now that you're graduating, don't you think you could finally pop the question?"

"Huh?" He looked at me as if I were nuts. "What do you mean?"

"You know what I mean, Josh. Everyone knows, for Pete's sake. You're in love with Caitlin."

It was fun watching his cheeks turn slightly red. And rather sweet too. But big brother was not about to fall for my tricks. "Did I tell you that I'm going down to Mexico for the summer again?" he said in an obvious attempt to change the subject.

"Yeah," I reminded him. "You e-mailed me about it."

"Well, I was thinking it would be really cool if Redemption could come down and do a little concert for the kids at the orphanage. I know it's a lot to ask. But there are a lot of teens down there that would really love it."

I thought about this. "You know, I just saw our summer schedule and we'll be down in California again in August. I could check with Willy and see if there's any way to squeeze something in."

"Cool. Let me know and I'll see that it's all set. Maybe we could invite people from the area too, charge for tickets, and if you guys were willing, maybe you'd like to donate the proceeds to the orphanage."

"You are a sly one, bro." I jabbed him. "And if you decide not to go into the ministry, maybe you could become an events manager."

"Isn't that what a pastor does anyway?"

"Speaking of pastors, it looks like Pastor Tony is waving to you, Josh."

"Yeah, I haven't even said hi to him yet."

"I'm going to go catch Caitlin." I watched his eyes at the mention of her name. Even if his life depended on it, I do not think Josh would be able to conceal his complete love, adoration, and affection for that girl. I just wish he'd get it over with and ask. But then he may be worried that she'll say no. She's already turned him down once. But I don't think she will the next time. As long as the timing is right. Now, I suppose that could be tricky.

"You getting all ready for the big tour?" I asked her after we hugged.

"I am so excited about this, Chloe. I can't believe that I actually get to do this. And get paid for it too. Man, I probably would've drained what little is left in my savings just to pay my way to come."

"Well, don't tell Willy or he might take you up on it. He's always looking for ways to cut expenses."

"That's fine with me. And I'll be happy to cook or clean or whatever it takes to keep you girls going."

"Wow, Elise made us do our own laundry and dishes and—"

"Hey, Caitlin," yelled Allie as she practically tackled the poor girl with a flying hug.

"Careful, Allie," I warned. "Caitlin was just offering to cook and clean and do all kinds of stuff for us. Don't injure her yet."

"Really?" Allie looked suspicious.

Caitlin smiled. "I was just telling Chloe that I'm so happy to be doing this tour with you guys that I'm willing to do whatever to make your lives easier."

"Sounds good to me." Then Allie glanced over to where her mom and Willy were chatting with Pastor Tony's wife, Stephanie Berringer. "Just don't tell my mom."

"Hey, I want to do whatever helps you girls to minister. I see myself coming on board as a servant."

"That's cool," I told her. "But you don't want to let us take advantage of you."

She nodded. "Don't worry. I'm meeting with Elise this week to hear about the details and stuff. She's making a list of everything I need to do."

Allie groaned. "Oh man, I knew my mom would mess this up somehow."

"Well, at least we don't have to do schoolwork during the summer tour," I offered.

"But we will be doing Bible study and devotions," Caitlin reminded us in a firmer-than-usual voice. "And just because you _think_ I'm so nice does not mean I'm a pushover."

We laughed. But there might be some people in this world who would try to push someone like Caitlin around. I mean, she is _so_ sweet and good.

But maybe that's why I don't think we will. She has the kind of heart where you really don't want to hurt her. I have a feeling we'll all try very hard to make her job easy. Now Beanie, well, that might be different. I think she can handle just about anything we care to dish up.

MEMORIAL DAY

we gather outside in the sun
to laugh and play and have some fun
hot dogs, sodas, tater chips
some are taking camping trips
but this day is for something more
time for those who've gone before
those who gathered in the sun
to laugh and play and have some fun
those who've left some empty spaces
those who are the missing faces
now we pause to think of them
to thank God that they're now with Him
where someday everyone will gather
our happy family back together

cm

Thirteen

Wednesday, June 1

I was surprised to get an e-mail from Jeremy today. Even so, I am trying not to make it into something it's not. He said he was thinking of me while working on a new song and wondered if I'd like to have a look at it. We've talked about song-writing a lot together, and I know this is simply a professional relationship. Okay, that sounds pretty lame. But Jeremy does respect me as a songwriter, and I'm honored that he wanted my opinion for his latest song, which is really quite good. I immediately let him know, along with a couple of minor tweaky suggestions.

I also know that I can trust his opinions on my songs—he usually has something very good to contribute to my writing process. We have a good working relationship that I plan to continue. And I think I can do this without getting my heart involved. Well, if I ask God to help me, that is. On my own, I would probably make a huge mess.

But at least I don't lay Iron Cross's CD covers all over my bedroom and go around gawking at Jeremy's photos and acting all lame and juvenile. Okay, Allie doesn't really do that. At least not when she knows anyone is looking. But even so, I have to give Al this: She's done a much better job than I have of keeping her heart under control. That has caused me to make this observation, which may or may not be correct. But I'm wondering if the girl who's all open and up-front about her feelings for a guy—acting all lame and gaga and whatever—is perhaps at less risk for getting hurt than the girl who hides her feelings, letting their roots grow deeply inside her but telling no one.

Okay, it's just a theory, so far. But it's also a good reminder to talk to my friends about this heart stuff. Like if I start going head over heels for Jeremy again, I will definitely talk to Allie and Laura, and even Beanie and Caitlin. And I'll ask them to pray for me and talk some sense into me. I also think it would be good for my pride because I have this disgusting habit of sometimes trying to appear more together and mature than I really am. But that is simply pride. And we all know where pride gets us in the end. Flat on our faces, or as Rosy would say, "Pride don't look good on you, girlfriend!"

THE FALL
it looks so good
at least at first
puffed up and full

then comes the worst
you think you're walking
straight and tall
then on your face
you flatly fall
into the mud
into the grime
you thought you'd pull
it off this time
but now you know
it never works
pride only makes us
look like jerks
so lay it down
at Jesus' feet
when pride is gone
life will be sweet
cm

Thursday, June 2

Okay, I know God wants me to love Tiffany Knight.
I mean, why else would she be stuck onto my life
like warm bubble gum plastered to the sole of a
flip-flop on a hot summer day? And time and
again I have tried to accept this as God's special
challenge for my life—loving the unlovable. So
why, I have to ask myself, do I want to run the
other direction every time I see her coming my

way? Like today in the cafeteria.

I was actually having a pretty good conversation with Kim Peterson—a girl who appears, at least to me, to be very spiritually hungry. Despite what she says in this regard, I get a strong feeling that God is at work in her. We'd started talking during fourth period and planned to continue it during lunch. I'd purposely chosen a quiet table off to one side where I didn't think anyone else would interrupt what was becoming a fairly serious conversation about faith.

"I'm not suggesting that religion doesn't work for you," she was saying just as Tiffany came over and sat down with us. "But it doesn't work for me. At least not the Christian version. But I may look into Buddhism someday, if I ever feel the need for some sort of organized religion."

"I'd have to agree with you about religion," I told her, nodding a polite "hey" in Tiffany's direction, although I secretly wished she hadn't joined us. "Because I happen to think religion is pretty stupid myself."

"But what about your songs?"

"I honestly don't think of them as religious, Kim. My music is more about my relationship with God. That's something completely different."

"I guess I don't really get that."

"Well, I've been going to youth group pretty

regularly for the last couple of months," inter-
jected Tiffany. "Actually, there's this really cute
guy there from McFadden who I like, but that's
another story. Anyway, I have to agree with Chloe
about the whole religion thing. Our youth pastor
says that Jesus came to do away with religion and
teach us how to have a personal relationship
with God." She glanced at me like the kid in
Sunday school who thought she should get a gold
star now. "Right, Chloe?"

I nodded. "And is that what you believe too,
Tiffany? Do you have a personal relationship
with God?"

She looked slightly puzzled just then. "Well,
I don't know. I guess so."

"You _guess_ so?" echoed Kim. "That doesn't
sound very convincing to me."

"I think I'm still figuring it all out," Tiffany
said with a slight frown.

Kim shook her head. "See, that's just the problem with religion. Why do you have to _figure_ it
all out?"

"That's what I'm trying to tell you, Kim." I
suppressed my exasperation at Tiffany's "helpful" input. I know it's not her fault that she's
still trying to "figure God out," and that's well
and fine, but I just wish she'd keep her "information" to herself if she's not really speaking from
personal experience. It'd be kind of like me

telling someone how to bake a cake from scratch—something I've never done in my entire life. Good grief!

Anyway, I reiterated to Kim that God is <u>not</u> something we can figure out with our heads, that it's a heart thing, and I explained how faith is a gift. But by then I think I was just wasting my breath. I suspect Kim doesn't like Tiffany any more than I do, and since Kim's not even attempting to follow God, I'm sure she has no interest in loving this somewhat obnoxious girl either. I wasn't a bit surprised when Kim excused herself and left me sitting alone at the table with Tiffany. But at least Tiffany acted like she was interested in my little sermonette.

"Hey, I totally love your new CD, Chloe," she said with bubbly enthusiasm. "I've been listening to it a lot."

I nodded and controlled myself from looking longingly over her shoulder to where Allie and Marissa had just sat with Cesar and Jake. "Cool."

And so it went, Tiffany and me hanging in the cafeteria, just the two of us. Oh my, what fun.

I watched David Letterman doing his Top Ten list last night. Yeah, I stayed up kind of late. But anyway, I'm thinking I should make a Top Ten list of reasons why I need to love Tiffany Knight. Okay, here goes nothing.

Top Ten Reasons for Loving
Tiffany Knight
(drumroll, please)

10. Because Jesus said to love our enemies.

9. Because if I don't love her, who on earth will?

8. Because it will teach me that if I can love her, I can love _anyone_.

7. Because it will make _me_ a better person.

6. Because it just might make her uncomfortable enough to bug off for a change.

5. Because she might feel guilty about being so mean to others.

4. Because I'm supposed to love my neighbors as I love myself.

3. Because she needs to experience unconditional love.

2. Because she might realize that God loves her way better than I can.

1. Because God is love, I belong to Him, and He will help me do this.

Wow, that was kind of cool. I actually began this little stunt thinking that I was going to write ten totally lame reasons, but then it started becoming the real thing. Now I feel as if I may be able to do this, with God's help, of course. I suppose it helps to know that school will soon be out, and we'll be leaving on tour by next week, so I won't be seeing Tiffany Knight for several months. Oh, I am such a coward.

DESPITE ME

i am so hopeless sometimes

so clueless and incapable

i think i have all the answers

but really i am a fraud

if i can't love the way You love

how can i call myself Yours?

if i can't be Your hands, Your arms, Your heart

how can i be anything worthwhile?

o God, despite my inability

my failures, my weaknesses

despite my selfish little self

please, love through me

wholly and purely and selflessly

love through me

despite me

touch the world and show Your love

amen

Fourteen

Friday, June 3

Laura graduated from Harrison High with honors today. Hip, hip, hurray! But even more amazing than that was the way she stood up to her mom. Not in a mean way, but simply in an honest and loving way.

Her parents were having a party for her after graduation. Naturally, Laura invited her band buddies to come, and everything was going just fine until Mrs. Mitchell let something slip.

"Laura could've been valedictorian, you know," she was telling a group of their church friends. "Up until this year she had a four point GPA."

"Mom," said Laura in an exasperated tone.

"Well, it's true," said her mom. "There's no shame in mentioning it, Laura. And if you hadn't been involved in your little rock band, I'm sure your GPA never would have dropped like it did this year."

Now, I could tell by that flash in Laura's dark eyes that she was ready to lay into her mom right then. But then I've never seen her be very disrespectful of her parents, and certainly not in front of a bunch of people. Still, there's always a first time. I, for one, was praying for her to stay in control.

"First of all," began Laura in a calm but surprisingly intense voice. "Redemption is not a little rock band."

Her mother smiled. "Well, there are only three of you."

"Right." Laura nodded. "But as far as that valedictorian business goes, I would far rather be a member of Redemption than to have stood up in front of Harrison High and given a speech tonight."

"But look at the influence you could've had for the Lord," said her mother. "I don't believe the valedictorian, Sarah Hardwick, was even a Christian."

"Excuse me," said Allie, stepping up importantly. "Perhaps you haven't noticed, Mrs. Mitchell, but Redemption has a fairly widespread influence for the Lord."

At least that made Laura laugh. "Yeah, Mom, we reach tens of thousands each month. By the end of summer we may have performed for a million." She glanced over to Willy. "Does that sound about right, Mr. Manager?"

He nodded. "Yep. And that's not even counting CD sales. I'd say you girls have a pretty good ministry."

"That is absolutely wonderful," said a woman from Laura's church as she patted Laura on the back. "And we are all so proud of you, darling."

An older man winked at Laura. "And don't let your mother get you down, honey. When you're not around, you should hear her going on and on about all the fantastic things you girls are doing."

Laura grinned. "Thanks, Mr. Howell."

And so it was all smoothed over. But I have to hand it to Laura for standing up to her mother. After all, Laura is eighteen, a high school graduate, and using her talents to serve God. I'd say the girl deserves some respect!

"Did you see what Rosy sent me?" Laura asked as the three of us girls went out into the backyard. She pulled out what appeared to be a framed photo and held it up.

"That is so cool!" exclaimed Allie.

I looked at the photo and laughed. "Hey, I forgot that Rosy took that."

"Remember, we were hot and tired and none of us had a key to the bus," said Allie.

In this classy photo, Allie, Laura, and I had all flopped down, hoping to shock Rosy when she finally came back to the bus. But there we were splayed out all over the sidewalk—arms and legs everywhere, mouths wide open with tongues hanging out, and eyes rolled back like we were having seizures. Very lovely.

"Wouldn't that make a great CD cover?" suggested Allie.

Laura laughed. "Yeah, I'm sure Omega would agree with you."

"Maybe it could be inside the CD case," I said. "I think it'd be hilarious. Like 'meet the real girls.'"

So we went and showed it to Willy, who does by the way have a nicely capped front tooth, and he thought it was a great idea.

"You girls," said Elise. "You really want everyone to know that you're crazy?"

Maybe so, I'm thinking. Maybe everyone should just lighten up and get a little crazy sometimes. And that, coming from a fairly serious girl like me.

GO CRAZY
sometimes you need to just go nuts
to lose your head and show some guts
sometimes you need to make things risky
to strut your stuff and just act frisky
sometimes you need to have some fun
to go outside and get some sun
sometimes you need to laugh then cry
to do what you're afraid to try
sometimes you need to run the race
even though it's a wild goose chase

sometimes you need to act deliriously
and not take life so doggone seriously
cm

Saturday, June 4

Another graduation. Today it was Josh. My parents and I drove up to his college and were totally blown away when Josh stepped up to the podium to give a speech. Okay, he wasn't valedictorian (and who cares anyway?), but he'd been selected by his classmates to give an inspirational message. I think that speaks quite highly of him. And I must admit that I felt proud. I think being proud of someone else isn't the same as being prideful about yourself. If I'm wrong, I'm sure God can correct me.

We went out for lunch afterward. I could tell that Josh was feeling a little low. I thought maybe he was sad to see this part of his education coming to an end.

"Are you sure you don't want to keep going until you have your master's?" asked my dad hopefully. This is a song he's been singing a lot lately. Being in the education field himself, I'm sure he feels a responsibility to especially encourage his own children to the highest levels of academia. Unfortunately for him, my oldest brother Caleb has absolutely no interest (at the moment). And I'm afraid I'm not too anxious to begin my college career, even if I do graduate from high school early.

"Like I already told you," said Josh. "I really feel I need to get out in the world a little before I go for my master's. I want some life experiences to add to my education."

"I think that's smart," I told him. "I personally like the idea of going to the School of Life."

Josh chuckled. "You're pretty lucky because your 'School of Life' actually pays pretty well."

"Yeah, but it could be over with by August."

"Willy told me that you girls have a really tough schedule this summer," said Josh.

I nodded. "We're really booked. Not only that, but a lot's riding on us now. The new CD just released, and Omega's expectation level is higher than ever."

My mom frowned. "I hope they're not putting too much pressure on you girls."

"It's okay," I reassured her. "We can handle it. God never gives us more than we can take."

"Just as long as you're sure that God's the One dishing it out," said Josh.

"I thought Caitlin would be here today," said my mom.

Now Josh frowned and I realized this was probably what was bumming him out. "Yeah, I thought she'd be here too," he said. "Apparently I was wrong."

"I know she's got a lot going on right now," I said quickly. "She just finished her finals and she's getting ready for our tour. Plus, I heard that her grandparents are visiting right now too. I'm sure she just got really busy."

He nodded and actually seemed relieved. "That's probably it."

"So, how are things going with you two these days?"

He shrugged. "I have absolutely no idea, Mom."

"Caitlin's a nice girl," said my dad. "But there's no point rushing these things, Josh. I don't claim to know that much about spirituality, probably not half as much as you kids do, but I do believe that God has perfect timing for everything."

I nodded. "So do I."

"Did I tell you that I heard from Caleb a couple days ago?" said Josh. "Everything's been so busy I almost forgot."

Naturally, we were all very interested and listened intently as Josh filled us in. Apparently Caleb has a decent job and recently got an apartment of his own.

"But the best part was that he's been going to Narcotics Anonymous," said Josh.

"That is so cool," I said.

"Do you think he'll stick with it?" asked Mom hopefully.

"We can all be praying."

"Well, this has been a moving day," Dad said as he actually blotted his eyes with his napkin. "First I get moved to tears by my son's amazing graduation speech. Next I hear that Caleb's doing better."

"Guess I shouldn't make any big announcements right now." I winked at Dad.

He shook his head. "Better save it for next time."

"You're always getting the limelight anyway," teased Josh.

"What? Are you jealous?"

"Sometimes I am," he confessed. "But then I realize you're doing what God has gifted you to do and there's no way on earth I could do that."

"And you're doing what God's gifted you to do," I reminded him.

So, I guess that settles it. At least two of the Miller kids are trying to follow God's purpose in their lives. And now it looks as though Caleb is actually making an attempt to get his life on track. I just pray that he lets God help him.

Fifteen

Tuesday, June 7

Ah, back on the road again. How I love this feeling. I wonder if I can even explain why it's so incredibly exhilarating. It's kind of like the carefree abandon of being a gypsy or a vagabond—singing for your supper. But in all fairness, this is paired up with a very serious feeling of responsibility. Does that make sense?

The carefree abandon part is being on the move, seeing new things, and not having to do much more than focus on music and performances. And of course, we have to stay focused on God too, and our relationships with each other. But those things are all pretty fun and fulfilling.

Now, the responsibility part is being ready—constantly ready—to be on stage and to do our very best. This can feel like a weighty load sometimes. But then I'm reminded to trust God. However, it doesn't feel like a weighty load today. Not with the big blue sky stretching over us and nothing but green fields on either side and a great long strip of highway leading us to our next concert. This is good.

AHHH
like a bird on the wing
how my heart wants to sing
as i soar 'cross the sky
flying high, flying high
like a fish in the sea
flip my tail with such glee
as i slip through the blue
feeling good, feeling new
like a horse running free
no reins or saddle shackle me
with the breeze for my friend
race the wind, race the wind
like a swan on the lake
carving a gentle wake
oh, such a lovely ride
as i glide, as i glide
cm

Monday, June 13

Wow, when Willy said this would be a demanding tour schedule, he wasn't kidding. But as I've told the others, we need to remember to pace ourselves. It's like we've just started running this marathon and we're not quite in shape yet. But if we give ourselves some time and grace, we should be able to keep up just fine. Anyway, that's my hope. I'm also praying that God will give us super strength.

I think out of all of us, Caitlin is holding up the best so far. She's like a tower of strength and energy. And she's still very excited about every single detail of this whole thing. It's fun to see, really.

"Where do you get it?" demanded Beanie yesterday morning when Caitlin was flitting around the living room of the hotel suite the five of us were sharing. She was happily opening drapes and straightening the room that still looked fairly trashed after our junk-food fest the previous night.

"What?" asked Caitlin.

"All that peppy energy," moaned Beanie from her spot on the couch. "You make me sick."

Caitlin laughed. "It's okay. Today's Sunday, our day of rest. Just take it easy."

We'd already decided not to go to church since we were singing for an evening service at some mega church that same night—as a promotion for our concert on Tuesday.

But Beanie popped out of her slump by noon. "I gotta go check out this retro store I noticed a couple of blocks down the street. Anyone want to come along?"

"Not me." Allie yawned. "I'm hanging by the

pool today. Doing basically <u>nothing</u>."

"Hoping to spot Brett?" I ventured.

"Is Iron Cross arriving today?" Caitlin asked as she picked up some discarded items of clothing.

"Yeah, they're supposed to get here this afternoon," said Allie. "Can't wait to see those guys. It feels like it's been ages."

"It's going to be so great to see both of your bands performing in the same concert," said Caitlin. "It's so exciting!"

Beanie made a silly face as she imitated her friend. "It's so exciting!"

Then Caitlin tossed a pillow at her. "Hey, excuse me for having a good time, but I happen to think this is fun."

"Yeah, so do I," said Beanie. "Just not with the energy level that you have. Now, does anyone want to go vintage clothes shopping with me?"

"I do," called Laura from the other room.

I was relieved because I was starting to feel guilty, like maybe I should offer to go, but I'm really not much of a shopper. Just ask my mom.

"I think I'll stick around and use this quiet time to work on some lyrics," I told them. And that's what I thought I would do. But the truth is, I ended up sleeping for most of the afternoon. Which, the way I see it, was probably smart since I was feeling pretty wiped from only one week on tour.

Then we did our promotional gig at the church and actually enjoyed a pretty decent sermon on how it's impossible to "outgive" God. And while I think this is absolutely true, I must express some disappointment that they decided to take another offering at the end of the service. I'm not sure why this bugs me. Maybe I think that if God's telling us to give, then we should just give, quietly and without much ado. I personally believe that God wants me to give generously—and I do, happily. But that's between God and me.

It was a relief the pastor had requested that no autograph session take place following the service. "If you want their autographs, you'll have to go to their concert with Iron Cross on Tuesday night at the auditorium." And that way, we were able to slip quietly back to our hotel and call it an early night.

"I'm going to go check for a package from Omega at the concierge," said Willy. "I'll see you girls bright and early for practice tomorrow."

"Yeah, bright and early," I tossed back at him. "Like around eleven?"

He gave me one of his Willy looks and then said, "Evening, ladies."

"Doesn't anyone want to stick around the lobby and look for the guys?" Allie suggested as we were heading toward the elevators.

"I don't think that's such a good idea," said Caitlin.

"Why not?" demanded Allie, pausing to put her hands on her hips as if a physical display might somehow help her sorry cause.

Caitlin seemed to consider this. I think this was the first time any of us had really put her on the spot. "Well, first of all, I don't think it's proper for young ladies to be hanging around hotel lobbies during all hours of the evening. And secondly, I think that if the guys from Iron Cross want to see you, they can call, and we can arrange some sort of acceptable meeting place."

"Huh?" Allie looked at Caitlin like she had two heads. "Did my mom tell you to act like this?"

Caitlin just laughed. "No. But she did tell me to keep a special eye on you, Allie, and to call her if you give me any grief."

Allie groaned. "It figures. Just when I get my mom out of the picture, I get stuck with Caitlin O'Conner, prison warden."

"Gee, thanks."

"It's okay," I told Caitlin in a quiet voice. "Allie didn't treat her mom any better."

"I happen to agree with Caitlin," Laura said as we went into the elevator.

Beanie leaned against the back wall and

rolled her eyes. "Caitlin's always been a little old-fashioned, but in the end, we all usually agree with the girl."

"Gee, it's so fun being the old ball and chain, the stick-in-the-mud," Caitlin said as she pushed the button for our floor.

"It's a tough job, but someone's got to do it."

As it turned out, we didn't hear from the guys last night at all. In fact, we didn't catch up with them until dinner this evening. But it was a happy reunion. They really do feel like family to us. I think it's because we have so much in common. We're basically living parallel lives, and whether we want to share success stories or complaints, we all pretty much understand how the others are feeling.

Well, almost. I'm pretty sure none of the guys from Iron Cross know exactly how I feel when it comes to their leader, Jeremy Baxter. In fact, I'm as surprised as anyone since I'd really tricked myself into believing that I'd gotten a handle on all this during our two-week break at home, and then even a third week this past week. But then I see him—those dark eyes, that serious expression, the way his hands gesture when he speaks—and suddenly all those old feelings come rushing in at me, like a tidal wave. And how do you stop a tidal wave?

SANDBAG MY HEART
prepare my heart
for the storm
keep me safe
keep me warm
heap those bags
around my heart
build that wall
before it starts
pile them up
and pile them high
keep me safe
keep me dry
before the waves
come rushing in
Lord, please, make me
strong again
amen

Sixteen

Saturday, June 18

Hardly a single day goes by where there's not something on the schedule. Sometimes it's only an hour-long commitment to sign CDs at a music store in a mall. Sometimes it's two concerts in one day. But it's safe to say we're all tired. And it's starting to show.

Allie and Laura got into a fight today. I don't think I've seen those two go at it since the early days when Laura thought Allie was a complete idiot for being interested in Wicca. Well, today Allie would be the first one to agree with her on that account. But they couldn't agree on where we should go for lunch. I mean, how stupid is that?

"I _want_ something junky and greasy," Allie was practically yelling when I came into the hotel room.

"Well, I don't," snapped Laura. "Man, don't you ever listen to your mom, Allie? Elise was always telling us about the fat content and empty carbs in fast food."

"Too bad, my mom's not here now." Allie flopped down in the chair by the window and pretended to pout.

"What's going on?" I asked.

"Allie's throwing a hissy fit because I don't want to eat at Burger Boy across the street."

"It's not a hissy fit."

"So why don't we just go our separate ways today?" I suggested.

"Because Willy wanted to meet us for lunch—all at the same place," said Allie in a dramatic voice. "And Laura wants to go to the stupid Garden Terrace—la-di-dah."

"And Allie wants to go slumming at Burger Boy."

"And I want to go use the bathroom." I shook my head. "You think you guys can sort this out while I'm gone?"

Apparently, they couldn't. Now they had Beanie and Caitlin involved, and it wasn't getting any better. Beanie had taken Laura's side. And Caitlin, even though she doesn't like fast food, was feeling sorry for Allie. Go figure.

Then the phone rang.

"That's Willy," said Allie. "Looks like you're the tiebreaker, Chloe."

I picked up the phone and told Willy we'd meet him at the hotel restaurant downstairs. I could hear the groans behind me, but I really didn't care.

"That's pretty creative, Chloe," Allie said in a snitty voice. "It's not like we don't eat half our meals in hotel restaurants."

"Look, Allie. You can get a burger and Laura can

get a salad. You should both be happy. It's just food, for Pete's sake!" Then I stomped out. Don't even ask me why. Maybe I just felt like being dramatic.

I think we all felt a little sheepish when we were seated at the restaurant table and Willy made his little announcement.

"Congratulations, girls. You now have two CDs on the bestsellers chart."

"No way!" I exploded.

He nodded. "Yep. Omega called this morning."

"That is so cool," said Allie.

"Awesome," said Laura.

Then the two of them did a cute little apology thing, and suddenly we were all friends again.

"Now the downside of this is that you girls will have to work really hard to keep this going," said Willy. "You need to stay focused and keep yourselves balanced."

"I've been meaning to mention this myself," said Caitlin. "I know I'm always the wet blanket around here, but I'm thinking each of you needs to be taking better care of yourself."

"How do we do that?" Laura asked as she took a bite of her salad.

"Like Willy says, that means balance. I'm talking about better routines. Going to bed earlier, getting a little exercise and fresh air, eating right." She eyed Allie's cheeseburger.

"Caitlin is right on," said Willy. "And as your

manager, I'm telling you to take this girl seriously. I don't know how someone her age got so much common sense, but you can thank the good Lord that He put her with us."

"I have to agree with Caitlin too," said Beanie. "The way you girls are living reminds me a little of my first year at college. I thought I could just go and go and keep on going. And before I knew what hit me, I was wiped out by Christmas. You girls have a really demanding schedule, and you've got to pace yourselves or you'll burn out."

We all sat there kind of stupidly nodding. I think we all know that they're absolutely right.

"So does this mean no more late night videos?" asked Laura.

Caitlin nodded.

"And no more junk food?" Allie looked crushed.

"Limited junk food," said Caitlin.

"And no more smoking and drinking and chewing?" I threw in just to be funny.

"That's right," said Caitlin. "It's time to clean up your act."

"Do we need to sign a contract?" asked Laura.

"I think your verbal agreement is good enough," said Willy. "After all, this is in your own best interest."

So we all sat there and solemnly promised to get serious about the program.

"And we need to encourage each other," said

Caitlin. "If we see someone struggling with a certain area, let's talk to her and pray for her and really be like the body of Christ."

I must admit I feel a certain sense of relief that we've come to this place. And I'm glad that Caitlin was strong enough to be the "bad guy" and call us to accountability. Because the fact is, we have two and a half months to go before we finish this thing. And I have a feeling we're going to need every ounce of strength and sanity to do it.

TRAINING DAYS
working out
getting strong
staying fit
going long
sweating hard
feel the pain
muscles ache
see the gain
going fast
keep the pace
this is how
you win the race
running hard
for that prize
the look that's in
your Father's eyes
cm

Sunday, June 26

Caitlin surprised me today. "Let's talk," she said after we'd all walked back from visiting a church near the hotel.

"Huh?"

"Just you and me, Chloe. Let's go have lunch together."

Laura had already announced that she was ordering room service and crashing with an old movie channel for the afternoon. And now it looked as though Beanie and Allie planned to join her, so I agreed.

We go to a Greek restaurant that Caitlin noticed yesterday. I'm not that familiar with Greek food but decide to trust her on this one.

"I want to say something to you," she says after they bring the first part of our meal out, cheeses and flatbreads all artfully arranged on grape leaves. "But I don't want to offend you."

I wave my hand. "Hey, go ahead, take your best shot. Is it bad breath? BO? Smelly feet? I can take it."

She laughs, then sobers. "Hey, I was trying to be serious."

I lean forward now. "What is it? What's wrong?"

"Okay, I'm probably sticking my nose into where it doesn't belong, but I think I've noticed something—something between you and Jeremy."

I sigh. "Sheesh, is it that obvious?"

"I'm not sure what you mean."

"I mean, is it that obvious that I'm still trying to get over my crush on him?"

She shakes her head. "No, that's not exactly what I mean. Oh, sort of. But I'm thinking this guy may have feelings for you too, Chloe."

I drop my piece of feta cheese and stare at her. "Are you nuts?"

"I don't know. And now I really do feel kind of stupid for bringing it up, but I just figured that you must've been aware of it, and maybe it was making you uncomfortable too?"

"This is too weird, Caitlin. I mean, I think you may be imagining something. Jeremy has a girlfriend, the same one he's had for about five years. I think they're going to get married. Kind of like—" I stop myself. I was almost going to say kind of like her and Josh, but then realized I'd probably just irritate her since every time I bring it up she seems a little distant, not to mention grumpy.

"Well, I don't know anything about a girlfriend, but I've seen the way Jeremy looks at you, how he talks to you, and I think something's up."

I shake my head. "Really, he thinks of me like a little sister, Caitlin. That is all, I guarantee it."

"I'm not so sure."

Now I start feeling this wild mix of emotions, and I almost think I'm going to cry. I'm not even sure why. "Caitlin!" I say loudly enough to get several pairs of eyes looking our way. Then I lower my voice. "Look, this is just what I DON'T need right now."

"What?"

"You, of all people, planting seeds in my mind about Jeremy."

Her hand flies to her mouth now. "Oh, Chloe, I did NOT mean to do that. I realize that you had feelings for him before, but I guess I thought you were over it now. And I felt worried that he might have feelings for you, and he's so much older, and I'd hate to see either of you getting hurt."

"Yeah, I can understand that. But don't you realize I've already been hurt..." I feel tears actually filling my eyes now. Stupid tears. I am so stupid. Or maybe I'm just tired.

"I'm so sorry, Chloe. I thought this was over and done with, at least on your end of things. Tell me what's going on with you now."

So I tell her the whole story. Not that I had a little schoolgirl crush that simply blew away, but how I feel like I have to deal with it over and over, and how often I pray about the whole thing and think I'm doing better, but then I see Jeremy and it all just seems to unravel again. And

Caitlin, as usual, is a very good listener. And what's really funny is how I actually feel better afterward.

"It's weird," I tell her. "I thought I was doing okay with all this—well, sort of okay. But it's like you just released some kind of pressure valve that needed to go off. The problem now is..." I wasn't sure how to put it.

"I've given you reason to think that Jeremy may be interested in you." She shakes her head. "Well, I'm sort of sorry, but sort of not. I guess what I'm doing is trying to warn you to watch yourself. I mean, Jeremy is a strong Christian and a perfectly nice guy. But it seems obvious to me that he thinks a lot of you."

I roll my eyes at her. "I just don't think—"

"Listen to me, Chloe. I can see it in his eyes when he's talking to you. He obviously respects you a lot, as a musician, a Christian, and a good friend. But I think there's something more too. I know that sounds kind of suspicious and slightly paranoid on my part, but I think it's my responsibility to watch out for you, Chloe. And I don't take that lightly. I mean I have no doubt that he's being really careful and telling himself to watch it. And I respect him as a mature Christian, but I just wanted to warn you. Okay? And hopefully you two can keep this thing under control."

"This thing?"

"Okay, let me cut to the chase, Chloe, because I want to be perfectly clear. As your chaperone and your friend, I do not want you to spend any time alone with Jeremy."

"Oh, Caitlin."

"I know, I know. I sound hopelessly old-fashioned and prudish. Tough. I am telling you that I do NOT want you spending any time alone with the young man. Do you understand me?"

I nod stupidly. "You're serious?"

"Absolutely. I know the chances of something happening are pretty minimal. After all, you're both strong Christians. But, you are both heading up some amazingly talented bands—bands with an incredible ministry for young people—and I'm sure that Satan doesn't like that a bit. He'd love to destroy both Redemption and Iron Cross, and what better way to do it?"

"Seriously?"

"And let's face it, Chloe, you're both passionate and creative people, and only human. And there will be days when you could both be pretty tired or disenchanted or lonely. Don't you see what I'm saying? Anyway, there's no sense in setting yourself up for what could become a really serious and devastating problem."

For the first time today, I seriously consider what she is actually saying to me. "Are you suggesting that you think it's possible that Jeremy and I could become romantically involved with each other?"

"Of course that's what I'm saying. Can you imagine the damage that would do to both of your bands and your ministries? This is the kind of thing that Satan could really have fun with."

I nod now as some of this sinks in. "Okay, Caitlin. I guess I can understand your concern. And maybe it is legit. I just highly doubt that Jeremy has any intention of sweeping me into his arms and laying a big one on me—let alone anything else you may be thinking."

"Then you are still a little naive."

"Thanks a lot."

"But you are also a dear girl, who I love like a sister and would do anything to protect."

"Thanks." And this time I mean it.

We talked a bit more, and Caitlin shared some of her various encounters with guys she had assumed were only friends and how easy it had been for someone to get the wrong message. "This is one of the reasons I still don't date."

I wanted to ask her if any of these stories involved my brother, but thought better of it. Everyone deserves a little privacy in some areas of their lives.

So tonight I'm still stewing over her little speech. I know she means well, but it sounds a little weird and slightly extreme to me. I mean,

Jeremy is a good guy—a great guy—and he'd never let anything happen between us. At least I don't think so. But then if I think about it too hard—and I'm trying not to do this—how would I really react if he did try something??? Now there's a good question. And to be perfectly honest, I am not sure. It has occurred to me that I'm not positive I could even trust myself if Jeremy came on to me. Because I know how much I like him. Who knows, I might even encourage him and initiate something myself. Okay, I don't really think I would do that, but on the other hand, things like physical attraction and hormones and chemicals are kind of unpredictable. And I know how deeply attracted I am to him. So I suppose there is a certain element of truth in Caitlin's theory. And I must admit that's pretty scary.

So whether Caitlin is right or all wet about Jeremy, I need to take her warning seriously for my own sake. And since I did promise her that I would never be alone with him again, I will adhere to that. And even if it is extreme and slightly paranoid, I have to ask myself, what's wrong with that? Wouldn't I rather be extreme and consequently avoid a pile of trouble than ignore my friend's warning and fall straight into a pit?

WORD TO THE WISE
when spoken in love
a good friend's word
brings health and life
when it is heard
counsel that's good
and kind and wise
can open your heart
and open your eyes
help me to trust
in the friends You give
to know they are here
to help me to live
a life that is right
a life that is true
a life that can give
all the glory to You
amen

Seventeen

Wednesday, July 6

This past week has been amazing. Amazing in that we're still functioning—because our schedule's been totally grueling—and amazing in what God is doing in and through us. Praise Him!

We've done six concerts in seven days. I can't even remember exactly where we were and when. But I do remember two days ago. We were performing with Iron Cross and several other Christian rock bands for a special Independence Day celebration in Bethlehem, Pennsylvania. It was an all-day concert with thousands of kids in attendance. And let me tell you, it was totally awesome.

We had as much fun being part of the crowd as we did performing. Probably even more so. Just rocking out with sisters and brothers in Jesus. So totally cool.

Then after it got dark, they had this humongous fireworks show, followed by an incredible worship time that I'll never forget. It was like a taste of heaven.

"I can't believe I'm getting paid to do this," Caitlin said as we rode in the limousine back to the hotel.

Beanie sighed. "I know what you mean."

"But you guys are both working hard," I reminded them.

"Maybe," said Beanie. "But not nearly as hard as you guys are."

"Hey, today wasn't so bad," said Allie. "It almost felt like a day off to me."

"Yeah," I agreed. "I could handle lots of days like today."

"Well, don't get your hopes up," said Caitlin. "Your schedule for next week is just as full as it was last week."

"But at least we get tomorrow off," Laura reminded everyone. "And I plan to sleep in until noon."

"As long as you make practice, you can sleep all day," I told her.

"No," said Caitlin. "Remember, we're trying to stay balanced. Laura can sleep in, but then she needs to get going."

Laura groaned. "You know, Caitlin, when you're done being our chaperone, you could probably get a job being an army sergeant."

"Yeah," said Allie. "I hear they're still recruiting."

Fortunately, Caitlin has gotten used to our ribbing her. And she's a good sport. Just the same, she is doing her best to keep us on track and balanced. For which we should be thankful.

GOD'S ARMY
we're marching for Him
and doing our part
our battle to win
we follow His heart
and though it gets tough
with enemy fire
even when it is rough
our spirits won't tire
until we are done
and victory waits
the battle is won
we're at heaven's gates

cm

Sunday, July 31

Well, our marathon is more than half over. I can't
believe I haven't written in my diary for so long—
weeks even! But that's only because time is so
precious. And here is how we spend it. We eat,
sleep, practice, and perform. And then we do it all
over again...again and again. Okay, I realize
some people probably think that being in a rock
band is glamorous and fun and exciting, but it's
really mostly a lot of hard work. It's a demanding
and seemingly endless job being on a concert
tour. And even after you're done with your performance, and it's getting late, and you're tired, and

all you can think about is finding a soft bed and being able to just sleep for about a week, it's time to meet the fans and sign autographs.

Even though I've gotten lots better about talking to fans, I still get weary and I suppose a little grouchy. When I'm really tired I can handle talking to someone who's hungry for God and wants to ask an important question. Like the girl last night.

"Hi, I'm Amy," she told me with a shy smile. She looked to be about my age, but very petite and sort of fragile looking.

Then as I signed her CD she asked me if she could ask me a question. Now, I was thinking "that's polite." And of course, I said yes.

"Well, I don't really like to talk about this, but I have leukemia."

That's when I noticed that the cool-looking bandanna around her head was actually covering up where her hair used to be.

"I'm sorry," I told her.

"No, that's okay. I'm pretty much used to it. And I realize that everyone has to die sometime." She paused and pressed her lips together, and I silently prayed that God would give me some sort of amazing words of encouragement, but mostly I just felt brain-dead.

"Anyway, I totally love your first CD. I listen to it all the time, especially the heaven song—

sometimes I play that one over and over. It's so encouraging. And, well, I was wondering, <u>how</u> did you write that song? I mean, did you just make it all up? Or do you think God inspired you? Or what?"

I had to really think about that. I mean, I wrote that song a long time ago. But suddenly it all came back. "You know what, Amy? I wrote that song in the middle of the night almost two years ago. And I was having this dream that seemed so real. It was about heaven, or that's what it seemed like to me. Anyway, I got up in the middle of the night and wrote down those words, which later became the lyrics to the heaven song."

"So, do you think God gave you that dream?"

"I guess I do. I mean, I don't really try to figure out where everything I write is coming from. I mostly hope it's from God, but then it seems kind of presumptuous on my part just to assume that everything coming down the pike is from God, you know what I mean?"

"But when I listen to your music, it feels like God is speaking to me."

"I know, and when I write lyrics and poems, it really does feel like God is speaking to me too. Still, I hate acting like I'm some sort of prophetess or something. I guess I just write what's on my heart."

"But do you believe God could be speaking to

me through your music? I mean, me personally?"

I smiled and reached for her hand. Giving it a squeeze, I said, "God spoke through a donkey in the Old Testament. I'm sure He could speak to you through me now."

She laughed. "Yeah. I thought so too."

"But we can weigh these things, Amy," I continued. "Like when we believe God's speaking to us through someone, we can go to His Word and see if it lines up with what we've heard. And then there's prayer too. God's spirit can give us a sense about things."

"Yes, that's what my pastor says too." She smiled. "But I do believe God speaks through your music, Chloe."

"Thanks." I squeezed her hand. "I'll be praying for you, Amy."

She nodded. "And I still believe that God could do a miracle if He wants. But I've just finished my last chemo, and it hasn't really worked. I wasn't even supposed to come here tonight, but I begged my mom." She glanced over her shoulder to where a middle-aged woman was waiting. I could tell by the look on her face that she was Amy's mother. And I could tell that she knew Amy didn't have long to live. I looked back at Amy, then gave her a big hug.

"I'm so glad you came tonight," I told her. "I think God is using you to speak to me. And in fact,

I'm feeling inspired to write a song about our conversation tonight. Would you mind?"

Her eyes grew wide. "Seriously? You're going to write a song about me?"

I nodded. "The words are already swirling around in my head. If you give me your address, I'll send it to you when I'm done."

So she quickly wrote down her address, which I pocketed, and we hugged again and I promised to be in touch.

Thankfully, my tears managed to stay in my eyes until she had gone, and the next girl in line didn't even seem to notice. Instead, she complained about how long it had taken to stand in line to get my stupid autograph, and that it was really for her little sister who was at summer camp, and she was only getting it because her mom wouldn't have let her come otherwise. "I'm not even into chick bands," she said, like that was her final insult. "The only reason I came tonight was to see Iron Cross. That Isaiah Baxter is so hot."

Well, it was all I could do not to write something mean and nasty in her stupid blue book, but then I reminded myself it was for her little sister. Besides, it probably wouldn't have seemed very Christlike to have used a four-letter word. Even if it was JERK.

So there you have it—the good, the bad, and

the ugly. Amy was the good, the impatient fan was
the bad, and I suppose I was the ugly when I
wanted to smack her in the nose. Well, I never
said I was perfect.

AMY'S SONG
a wisp of a girl
she stood in line
with clear blue eyes
that saw through mine
and when i looked
into her face
heaven was there
mercy and grace
although young
her soul was old
she'd been through fire
like burnished gold
i saw my Lord
i saw His touch
upon this child
He loves so much
and that is when
i realized
that Amy has
heaven's eyes
cm

Eighteen

Friday, August 12

I'm afraid I've blown it. Really, really blown it. I know I need to tell someone, and I will, but it's late right now and everyone but God is in bed. And I've already told God that I'm sorry, but He's not saying much. So for now, it seems I'll have to bear this burden alone.

I can make lots of excuses, all kinds of excuses. Like this concert tour is too long and hard and demanding, like I'm human and under a lot of stress, like I'm only seventeen and trying to take on the responsibilities of an adult, like I'm tired of being a Christian role model for thousands of girls who make mistakes like this all the time. And all my excuses sound good and believable. At least to me.

Caitlin warned me to watch myself and my relationship with Jeremy. And mostly I have. Oh, I still talk to him and we compare notes on songs and stuff. But I've made a special effort not to put myself in any "compromising" situation with him—as in we don't hang out just the two of us. I was almost beginning to think that we had some sort of unspoken agreement, although we never discussed this. That would be too stupid. Because really, I never thought Jeremy would do anything. He is, after all, Jeremy Baxter, lead singer for the number one Christian rock band in the country. He's won music awards and performed around the world. Why would he: 1) want to jeopardize that by getting involved with a seventeen-year-old? or 2) have any romantic interest in me in the first place? The whole idea seemed preposterous.

And the more time that went past, the more I thought that Caitlin was just being one of those paranoid Christians who thinks everything is scary and evil. Oh, I'm exaggerating there, she's not really like that. I guess I just thought, "Hey, I'm Chloe Miller, I'm in control, and I'm above doing anything stupid, anything that would risk our reputation or the tour." I suppose it was a case of pride getting the upper hand. You'd think I'd know better.

But back to my excuses, there's someone else I could blame just a little. (I know this is a silly game, but I need to play it just now.) Beanie has been slowly changing my image from grunge girl to urban sophisticate. And since everyone says it's an improvement, I've been playing along. The result of this is that I look a little more like a girl. I don't get away with wearing cargo pants and T-shirts and Doc Martens all the time. "Your uniform," as Allie used to say.

And they've all encouraged me to let my hair grow out, and it now reaches to my shoulders and looks kind of shaggy and cool. And okay, I'll go so far as to say that I'm looking pretty good this summer. I'm not a beauty, but as Beanie says, "You're growing into your looks." Well, whatever. But this probably has given me a little more confidence when it comes to guys. Because I've noticed that guys pay more attention to me than they used to—I mean, besides the music part of my life. I get plenty of attention in that arena.

Oh, I'm sure I could go on and on and keep this up until morning without ever really putting down here what happened. And my whole point in writing this down was to make myself better. I think that when I see what happened in black and white (okay, purple and white since that's my ink color tonight) I'll see that it's not really so bad. Not the end of the world as we know it. And maybe I can even just quietly sweep the whole thing under the rug, pretend it never happened, and return to life as normal. Okay, I realize I'll need to talk to Jeremy about it and make sure that it never happens again. But I can do that. I _must_ do that.

So here's what happened. We'd just finished our concert (the first one we'd done with Iron Cross in a week), and the lingering group of groupies had dwindled to about a dozen or so, mostly girls wanting to get signatures from the guys, although Allie and Laura were chattering away with several too, and I realized this could still go on for another thirty minutes. Anyway, feeling totally beat and useless, I slipped backstage to where I'd earlier spotted a couch that looked to be about a hundred years old. And I thought I'd just take a quick nap. No biggie. I'd barely stretched out on it when I heard footsteps and looked up to see Jeremy. Again, no biggie. We all know our way around the back of a stage by now.

"Hey," he said. "That's exactly what I was going to do."

I sat up and made room for him. "Great minds, you know."

He smiled. "It's been a busy summer for you girls. How you holding up?"

"I guess we're doing okay." I reached around and rubbed a sore spot in my left shoulder—playing guitar every night can mess with your muscles. "But I'm sure we could all use a good, long rest."

"Your neck hurting you?"

I nodded. "Do you get that too? That thing right between your shoulder blades after a long night."

"Yeah. Turn around."

And so I did. And Jeremy began gently massaging the muscles around my neck and shoulder blades. And man, did it ever feel good. At first it was just the therapeutic touch on my sore muscles, but within moments, seconds even, I realized that I was feeling something else too. Something dangerous. But instead of listening to the little voice inside of me (the one that sounded just like Caitlin O'Conner tonight), I just sat there and soaked in all these amazing feelings.

"It's been fun watching you girls growing up on this tour," he said as he worked his thumbs in little circles around my spine.

"Growing up?" I queried, mostly just to keep him talking and rubbing my neck. Okay, I am shameless.

"Yeah. When I found out that Redemption was going to open for us, I was a little concerned. I thought you girls were too young. The truth is, I was a little insulted that Omega had paired us with you in the first place. But then I heard you play."

"And you decided you could hang with the kiddies as long as they knew how to perform?"

"Exactly." He laughed. "And you girls have continued to impress me throughout this whole year."

"Well, thanks."

He kept rubbing. "Thank you."

Then it was quiet, and I began to feel pretty

uncomfortable. Okay, I was feeling pretty good too, excited and just a little light-headed and crazy.

"I really respect you, Chloe," he said in a quieter voice. "And I don't know if you've noticed or not, but I like you a lot too."

I could feel my heart starting to pound now, so loud, I was sure that Jeremy could hear it too.

"And it's even starting to bug me that you're only seventeen."

He stopped rubbing my shoulders, and I turned around to stare at him. "What?"

He smiled a funny smile. "Or maybe I wish I was Isaiah's age."

I'm sure the look on my face was somewhere between stunned speechless and oh-man-I-wanna-kiss-your-face!

"I'm sorry," he said quickly. "That was out of line."

I shook my head. "No, it wasn't, Jeremy. I mean, I wasn't going to say anything to you, but I've wished the same thing since I first met you."

"Really?"

I nodded. I think I actually thought I might've been dreaming just then. I thought maybe I was actually snoozing on the dusty old couch and just having this way cool dream.

"I broke up with my girlfriend."

I felt my eyes growing wider. "Really?"

"Yeah. I knew that something had to be missing if I was spending more time thinking about you than her."

"No way!" And then I did something totally stupid. I threw my arms around him and the next thing I knew we were kissing. K-I-S-S-I-N-G! Passionately kissing, kissing, kissing, for several minutes that actually felt like several hours or maybe just a few fleeting seconds—oh, how do you know these things for sure?

I can feel my face burning even now just to be writing this down. But to be honest, my cheeks are probably burning with lust just as much as from embarrassment. I am, after all, only human.

Fortunately, we both realized what was happening and pulled away almost simultaneously. I could tell by the look on Jeremy's face that he was just as shocked as I was.

"I'm sorry," I said. "I shouldn't have—"

"No, no, I'm the one who should be sorry, Chloe. I didn't mean for—"

"Chloe!" It was Laura's voice yelling for me. Thankfully she was still around the corner.

"I gotta go," I whispered as I stood and ran to find Laura.

And that was that. Oh, I know I'll have to talk to Jeremy. And I'm not even that worried about it. Of course, I realize there is no way we can continue a relationship like that. Okay, my mind knows this. My heart is singing a different tune.

The hard thing is going to be telling Caitlin, especially after she warned me. But at least she might have the satisfaction of saying, "I told you so." Not that she's like that. She's not. But I deserve it.

Still, even though I know I blew it, the weird and confusing part is feeling this crazy mix of emotions right now. I'm not even sure I can list them, but I'll try.

1. Embarrassed. I thought I had more self-control.
2. Thrilled. To think Jeremy really has feelings for _me_!
3. Humbled. I really am only human.
4. Ecstatic. Jeremy broke up with his old girlfriend—for me!
5. Confused. I am only seventeen. How can I have such serious feelings?
6. Flabbergasted. The most amazing guy on the planet likes _me_!
7. Humiliated. To think I broke my pact with Allie and Laura. Big-time.
8. Dreamy. I wonder when we'll get married. What will I wear?
9. Stupid. What am I thinking? I'm too young to get married.

10. Hopeful. Maybe if we both can wait, maybe God can work it out.
11. Lame. Why did I let this happen now? What about my music?
12. Repentant. I'm sorry I didn't wait for God on this.

Now, as I said, I already confessed this all to God, and I know that He forgives me. And I know that what happened tonight, as long as it remains an isolated event, won't jeopardize anything for our bands. I also know that I will do everything I can to make sure it doesn't happen again. But God is going to have to help me a lot with that.

MESSES

i disobey

and make a mess

and then it's time

to confess

but why I didn't

do it right

is why i am

awake tonight

cuz if i'd done it

with God's blessing

it wouldn't make

such a messing

if i'd honored

God's best way
i wouldn't dread
the break of day
cm

Nineteen

Sunday, August 14

Because we had an afternoon concert yesterday, I had to wait until the evening to have my conversation with Caitlin. I'd decided to talk to her first (before Allie and Laura) and see what she recommended for me.

But before any of that happened, I woke up (after about three hours of sleep) to find an envelope slipped under the door. It was the hotel stationery and addressed to me. I opened it up to find it was from Jeremy. I am taping this letter into my diary. It feels like one of those mementos that I will treasure always.

Dear Chloe,

I am so sorry that I took advantage of you last night. I never meant for that to happen and am not even sure how it did. But I do take the full blame. Please, forgive me.

As you know by now, I do have feelings for you. You're the coolest girl I know and I love being with you. I love your creativity, your passion for life, and most of all, your heart for God. However, we both know that this thing between us is not going to happen <u>right now</u>. There's too much at stake, and way too many people depending on us, to let this thing get out of hand.

I feel horrible that I let my feelings get away from me last night. Still, it's a good reminder that I'm only human and perfectly capable of messing up. Thank God for His mercies, which are new every morning! But if we're going to have a relationship, I must take the lead and let you know that I will be waiting for God's timing in this and in all things.

I may not get a chance to talk to you tomorrow, but if you look in the envelope, you'll see a leather wristband. I know it's kind of outdated with the old WWJD burned into it, but a good buddy gave it to me back in middle school. If you can forgive me and want to continue our friendship at a safe distance, please wear this tomorrow and I will feel reassured. And if I've really stepped over the line and messed us up for good, well, I just hope we can talk later.

Forgive me,
Jeremy

Oh, my heart felt so much better after reading that. Sure, I was still irked at myself, but at least I knew that Jeremy and I were on the same page. And I put on that wristband and wore it all day. I may wear it for the rest of my life, if Jeremy lets me keep it. But I'll understand if he wants it back, especially since an old buddy gave it to him. And I do not think the WWJD is outdated. Good grief, I could've used this kind of guidance on Friday night when we were indulging in our big make-out session. It still scares me to think what would've happened if someone, like a music critic or anyone with a big mouth, had caught us like that. The spin they could've put on a story like that would've hurt us all.

I have to hand it to Caitlin. After I told her my story, she didn't even get mad or say "I told you so." But I could tell she was disappointed in both me and Jeremy.

"I'm really sorry, Caitlin. Believe me, I do wish I'd listened to you better. And actually I had been taking your advice pretty seriously, but then last night just sort of happened. It was weird."

She nodded. "Yeah. It is weird. That's what I was trying to tell you. When you really like a guy and he likes you...well, one thing leads to the next, and before you know it, you're thinking about going to bed with him."

"Oh, I wouldn't—"

"Hey, Chloe." She gave me the eye now. "That's what you said the last time we talked, remember?"

I shrugged.

"It's way easier said than done, isn't it? And I know because I've been there. And I've had friends who've been there. And even though it feels wonderful and natural and beautiful at the time, it almost always blows up in your face eventually. Physical intimacy almost always leads to sexual intimacy, and sexual intimacy before marriage will always set you up for serious problems."

Well, I wasn't about to challenge her on this one. The funny thing was, I think she wanted me to. I think she was all ready to give me another little speech. But I guess she decided to save it for today. We girls had decided to have a partial day of rest by hanging at the hotel until it was time to hit the road at noon. And Caitlin was going to lead us in a devotional, but instead of doing our regular book, she did a devotional on sexual abstinence. Naturally, she had to tell the others that this was my fault. And of course, that required an explanation.

"Why don't you tell them what's going on, Chloe?"

Well, you could've heard a pin drop in our room, and that's with thick plush carpeting. So, knowing she was right, since she'd told me that it was going to take all of us working together in honesty to prevent something like this from happening again, I told them about Jeremy and me.

When I was finished, they all looked stunned. Well, except for Caitlin. But I think Beanie's mouth was actually hanging open.

"Now, you guys have to keep this confidential," said Caitlin. "And the reason I encouraged Chloe to share this was so that we could all support her in her commitment not to let this happen again."

"You won't, will you?" said Laura. "I mean, it could really mess things up for both our bands. Jeremy is a grown man and you're still a teenager."

Okay, that irritated me. "But it would be okay if Jeremy liked you," I said. "Since you're eighteen."

Laura smiled. "Well, I wouldn't want to make you jealous."

I threw my sandal at her.

"It does seem funny, doesn't it?" said Beanie. "That this is such a problem because of your ages."

"There's more to it than that," said Caitlin. "Both bands are constantly in the public eye to maintain the high standards that they represent in their music ministry. It's only fair that they live up to them in their personal lives."

"But what if they're really in love?" said Allie. "What if God wants Jeremy and Chloe to get married?"

"Maybe He does," said Caitlin. "But God still has a perfect timing for these things, and I suspect Chloe's parents wouldn't agree to it, at least not before she turns eighteen and graduates from high school."

"I know something like this would freak my mom out," said Laura.

"And do you think it would do anyone any good if Jeremy and Chloe started getting serious, like dating and kissing and getting more involved?"

"Maybe if Chloe were eighteen," said Allie. "It wouldn't matter so much then, would it?"

Caitlin smiled and we all knew this was her cue to begin her little speech. I knew that, because of me, we would all be forced to listen like a captive audience (the kind who are actually bound and gagged). But in the end it wasn't really so bad.

"I've taught this to a number of girls' groups," she said. "And under the circumstances, it seems appropriate to share it again."

"Did you know we used to call her Preacher?" whispered Beanie, and the three of us laughed.

"Make fun if you want," she said. "But truth has a way of standing up to abuse."

Then she began talking about herself and how

she'd been in situations where what started out as a simple kiss quickly moved to a groping session that ended up with her feeling pressured to have sex. "Everyone else is doing it," she said. "That's one of the most common excuses you'll hear. That and 'you'll do this if you love me.' But think about it, do either of those make sense? First of all, everyone else is NOT doing it. Oh, sure, lots of kids are. But there are a lot who are keeping their heads, having a healthy life, serving God, getting ready for their futures, and not having sex. But it's the second one that always gets me—you'll do it if you love them. Well, how selfish is that?" She turned to Beanie. "You want to contribute anything here?"

And to everyone's surprise, Beanie stole the show. She told us how she'd gotten involved with a guy during her junior year of high school, fallen head over heels in love, and been talked into having sex.

"It wasn't even that fun," she admitted. "But I thought it would make us closer. I thought it would show him I loved him. We were both Christians, and I honestly believed it was God's will for us to be together forever. Having sex just seemed to seal it."

"And did it?" asked Caitlin, but in a tender voice.

Beanie shook her head. "If anything, it drove

us apart. It ruined our relationship completely and even caused him to fall away from the Lord." Her eyes actually filled with tears now.

"Why?" asked Allie.

"Well, for one thing, I got pregnant."

The room got even quieter.

Beanie took a deep breath. "Zach was a senior and had been offered a full athletic scholarship for track, and the last thing he wanted was a pregnant wife dragging him down. He dumped me faster than a worn-out pair of Nikes."

"Oh, man," said Laura.

"Yeah. I got so depressed that I even considered suicide. It just felt like my whole life was over. Like I'd lost everything and had nothing left to live for."

I nodded, swallowing the lump that was steadily growing in my throat. I'd never known any of this about Beanie and felt honored that she was sharing so much with us now.

Caitlin had taken Beanie's hand. "But God was there for you, right, Beanie?"

She smiled. "God and Caitlin and a couple of other good friends."

"What happened to the baby?" asked Allie.

"I lost it."

"She lost it," continued Caitlin, "when she got hit by a car in order to protect my little nephew."

"Oliver?" said Allie. "You saved Oliver?"

Beanie nodded.

"Wow." Laura shook her head in amazement.

I think all three of us were pretty moved by Beanie's story. So much so that Caitlin let us off easy. "The main thing is," she said, "I really believe God wants us to respect ourselves and our bodies. He wants us to keep ourselves pure for our wedding day, not to punish us, but so that we can enjoy a marriage relationship completely unhindered. When you've slept with other people, you end up dragging a bunch of emotional crud into your marriage—old hurts, insecurity, inability to trust. And from what I've heard, it can really mess with your sex life too. I mean, think about it—if you really love your husband, do you want for him or you to haul all your ex-lovers into the bedroom with you?"

We laughed about that. But I think I understand what she means. I know that when I get married (and okay, I hope and pray it will be with Jeremy), I don't want either of us to have old "stuff" to deal with. Most of all, I'd rather we do things God's way and as a result enjoy a really good relationship with each other. And I know that means waiting. In our case, due to our music and ministry, there really are no options. I understand this. And I have decided, once again, that waiting may not feel good, but it's way better than messing everything up.

WAIT ON GOD
God's clock is not ours
it goes its own pace
sometimes it's so slow
sometimes it's a race
sometimes we are waiting
and wondering when
and praying and hoping
we almost give in
but if we are patient
and wait til it's time
the reward will be worth it
and all will be fine
cm

Twenty

Friday, August 19

Jeremy and I met for lunch today. Caitlin said it was okay because we were meeting in a public place. Besides, we needed to talk and get everything squared away. I can't believe how nervous I was. You'd think I was getting engaged or something. Which I know is perfectly ridiculous. Caitlin has really been coaching me about how it's important for Jeremy and me to remain good friends. But <u>only</u> friends.

"Any lasting relationship, especially marriage, is built on a good solid friendship," she told me a couple of days ago. "If you're not best friends with a guy, and if you don't really know him and LIKE him—I mean <u>like</u> just hanging with him, talking with him, listening to him, having similar interests and goals as him—well, you shouldn't even <u>think</u> about marriage." Then she laughed. "Not that you should be thinking about marriage anyway."

To further drive home her point, she told me about Anna, an African-American girl I remember vaguely, but I knew she'd been good friends with

Caitlin and Beanie and Jenny during their senior year.

"Anna fell in love during her senior year in high school. I mean, we're talking IN LOVE. She was absolutely nuts over this guy named Joel. And she and Joel continued dating into college. But it wasn't long before Anna was obsessed with the idea of them getting married. She says now that it may have been due to the fact she never had a dad, and this could be true. Anyway, even though Joel loved her, he still really wanted them to finish college first. They were both really smart with bright futures ahead. But Anna kept pressuring him, even to the point of introducing sex into their relationship."

Caitlin paused. "The only reason I'm telling you this is because I think Anna would agree that there's a powerful lesson here. Anyway, Joel finally gave in to getting married. Anna said it was mostly because he felt guilty that, as Christians, they were having sex outside of marriage. So they got married last year, and Anna had to quit school to help support them. She's working at a Wal-Mart right now. And the last time I talked to her, she was so bummed. She said that she hardly ever sees Joel, and when they're together they fight most of the time. She's seriously worried their marriage might not survive."

"That's sad."

Caitlin nodded. "That's what I thought too. I encouraged Anna to get her life back on track—I mean with God—and I suggested they get some kind of counseling, but Anna said they don't have time and can't afford it. Anyway, I'm really praying for them. You can too, if you think about it."

"Yeah. I will. Maybe I can remember to pray for Anna and Joel the next time I get caught up in thinking about how wonderful it would be to marry Jeremy."

"That's a good idea. Because I would strongly warn you about controlling your thoughts when it comes to Jeremy, Chloe. I think that's how Anna got so obsessed about Joel. It's like she thought about him night and day. She didn't put her energy into school and friends and, well, look where it got her."

I hugged Caitlin then. "I am so glad you're our chaperone, Caitlin. I'm so thankful that God sent you to tour with us right when He knew I would need you the most."

"God's pretty amazing."

So today it was lunch with Jeremy. Okay, I must confess I dressed with more than my usual care, going through about eight outfits before I settled for a denim skirt and a peasant top (not my normal hanging-out uniform of cargo pants and T-shirt). I tried to do this so that no one else noticed, but just as I was going out of the hotel room, Allie glanced up from the book she was reading.

"Looking good, Chloe." Then she winked at me. "Now, don't do anything I wouldn't do."

I frowned at her. "Like what's that supposed to mean?"

She laughed. "I don't know. I just thought it sounded good. But really, I'll be praying for you."

"Thanks." And I meant it.

Jeremy was waiting for me in the lobby. "We can eat in the hotel restaurant, if you'd prefer, or there's a little sushi bar down the street. Do you even like sushi?"

"Actually I do. It took a couple times before I developed the taste for it, but now I like it."

He smiled. "Somehow I thought you would."

As we walked out of the hotel, I confessed to him how nervous I was.

"I know it's stupid," I told him. "But this all just feels so, well, surreal to me."

He nodded. "Yeah. Me too."

But after we were seated and drinking some green tea, I began to relax. I told myself this was no different than all the other times I'd hung with Jeremy. Okay, it was a little different.

"Sorry we haven't been able to talk sooner." He pointed to the wristband I was still wearing. "But when I saw you wearing that last Saturday, well, I figured we were basically okay. Basically."

I ran my finger over the letters on the band. "I've been wearing it ever since you gave it to me." I looked up at him. "Do you want it back now?"

"No. I want you to keep it."

"Thanks." I allowed myself one brief look into his eyes, then almost regretted it. A girl could get lost in those dark pools.

"I considered e-mailing you during the week," he continued. "But I thought I'd rather talk to you in person, and I knew we'd be meeting up here in Cincinnati for the concert tonight."

"No problem. It was kind of nice having a week to process things. And Caitlin has been like my personal counselor. She's so wise."

"Yeah, she's a cool girl. She seems pretty level-headed."

I glanced at him nervously, worried that perhaps he found Caitlin more attractive than me. Okay, so I'm pretty insecure.

"In fact, Caitlin reminds me a lot of my old girlfriend."

I nodded and took a sip of tea. Now where was this going, and why was I suddenly feeling so jealous and territorial?

"Do you mind if I tell you a little bit about Tracy, my old girlfriend?"

"Not at all. I'm actually pretty curious." Now this was mostly true, yet at the same time I felt like I was about twelve years old and shrinking steadily.

"Good. I feel like I need to explain this to you, to sort of clean the slate. Or maybe I just want to for my own sake. Anyway, Tracy and I had gone together since high school. I was a serious Christian and not interested in dating anyone who wasn't. Tracy fit the bill. She'd been raised by fairly conservative Christian parents, not too different from my own. She was committed to God and basically just a really nice girl. Not unlike Caitlin."

"A rock."

He smiled. "Yeah, you got it. Tracy is a rock. And that's not a bad thing either. I really admire her. But when I met you..." He shook his head as if he still wasn't too sure about this whole thing, but then he continued. "All I could think was, wow. I was so impressed by your energy and spunk. I was amazed by your creativity and felt challenged by your passion for God and life. I loved how you question so many things, how unconventional you are, your innate understanding of music...oh, so many things, Chloe. Am I gushing here or what?"

I laughed. "Hey, it's okay with me. I could listen to this for decades."

"Like I told you, the age difference really blew my mind. I knew it would never work—I mean,

I didn't even intend for it to work. I know how people, like Omega or reviewers or even some fans, would have a fit." He looked down at his little cup of tea and shook his head. "Did you know that Eric Green had actually given me this speech before we met you girls? He told me to keep an eye on the younger guys in my band, in case they decided to put the move on any of you girls."

I laughed again.

He smiled. "Little did Eric know that I would pose the greatest threat. Man, I didn't even know it myself. So after I met you, I realized right away that I had to watch my step. So I decided to play big brother with you, to take you under my wing and enjoy your company and friendship, but to keep it all under great control."

I nodded. "That's exactly what I kept telling myself too. I mean, that I was just your little sister. Problem was, my heart wouldn't listen."

"Yeah. I know what you mean. Finally, I realized that even if I couldn't do anything about pursuing you—and I knew that I couldn't—I should at least be honest with myself and Tracy and break things off. I knew that I couldn't possibly love her if I was feeling that attracted to someone else."

"How did that go with Tracy?"

He ran his hand over his already smooth hair. "I'd like to be able to say it went really well, that

she understood perfectly and was ready to move
on with her life."

"But she wasn't."

"No way. She was actually pretty ticked at me.
But consequently she said some things that reassured me that I wasn't making a mistake in
breaking up. I mean, she's a cool girl and a strong
Christian, but she's not right for me. And I'm not
right for her. I think she'll realize that in time."

"I hope so."

"And now we're here." He sighed. "And I'm sorry
because I really hadn't meant to rush us into
anything. I honestly thought we could continue
being friends; I'd wait until you got a little
older, like at least eighteen." He peered at me.
"When do you turn eighteen anyway?"

I laughed. "Not until March 3."

"That's not too bad. Besides that, we both have
our music. That's enough to keep us occupied and
out of trouble, right?"

"And we can still continue being friends?"

"I hope so. I just know that I'm going to have
to really watch myself."

"Me too."

His smile seemed laced with sadness now, or
maybe it was regret. "I just don't get why God did
it this way though. Bringing us together when we
both know there's nothing we can do about it. It
doesn't make a lot of sense."

"Sometimes I almost think I get it. Then other times I'm not so sure..." I didn't mention how I just about drowned in his eyes only moments ago and would've given anything to have my birth certificate read differently. Instead I continued, "But this is what I think it's about. At least for me. I think God wants me to grow in Him. And He's not going to insulate my life from troubles, because that's usually what makes me grow the best. Not that I see you as trouble, Jeremy." I shook my head. "But with you in my life, I realize I'll have to practice a whole lot of self-control, I'll have to become more mature and focus myself to keep my mind on God, I'll have to be continually surrendering my will to His. It's almost overwhelming."

"I've had some of those same thoughts. And I've got to admit that this whole thing has been kind of humbling. It's a good reminder that I really don't have things under control and that I need to fall hard on God."

"I know what you mean. It's good for us, but it's not very easy."

"I've heard that the best things in life never come easily."

"Or quickly."

He grinned. "You got that right."

It was all I could do at that very moment not to leap from the stool and throw my arms around him, kiss him, and tell him I loved him. But thank God, I didn't. I am exercising a little self-control—or a lot, depending on where you're standing.

"So, do you think we're up for this kind of challenge?" he asked.

"I am if you are." Then I thought of something. "Do you think we should make some sort of agreement?" Now I wondered if this was going to sound silly or juvenile, but I decided to just plunge in. "I mean, something that will help us to do this thing God's way without compromising or messing things up. Like in our band, we all signed this pact saying we would not let guys interfere with our music ministry. It's a way to call each other to accountability, and so far it's working."

"That's a very cool idea."

"A very necessary idea. A year ago, I would've thought an agreement like that had more to do with Laura and Allie since they were both struggling through relationships. But now I think it was mostly for my sake. Like you said a minute ago, it's all pretty humbling."

"But that pact is a great idea. Maybe I should work up something like that for the guys."

I felt one of my brows lift slightly. "The guys?"

"Or maybe just for me."

I laughed.

"But you're onto something, Chloe. I think we should have some sort of agreement between the two of us."

So we sat there discussing it for a bit until we had the language down. Then Jeremy wrote it out in his neat printing on a paper napkin, then made another copy for me. This is what it says:

We, Jeremy Baxter and Chloe Miller, do hereby agree to continue our friendship only as long as God remains in the center of our relationship and is glorified by our lives. If our relationship distracts us from God, we both hereby agree to terminate it at once.

Then we both signed and dated the two copies and shook hands. It was hard letting go of his hand, but somehow I managed.

"Agreed?" His eyes locked with mine.

"Agreed." God help me, I was thinking.

I am now taping this napkin document into my diary. I consider it to be legal and binding, and I intend to honor it with every ounce of my strength. Thankfully, I fully believe that God will help me when my strength is not enough. Because the truth is, I don't think I could possibly carry off something like this on my own. I know my weakness. I am well aware of my human frailty and limitations. I'm not a fool. So, I go into this with God at my side, holding His hand, and trusting that He will see me through—for His glory!

PROMISE
a vow to God
is a vow to keep
a promise made
will not come cheap
shake hands with God
and give your word
that you will do
what He has heard
to God alone
you must be true
don't kid yourself
He sees through you
so hold on tight
focus your eyes
stick to your vow
and win the prize!
cm

Twenty-One

Saturday, August 27

The past week has been a mixed blessing. We've been so busy traveling and performing that I've hardly spoken more than a couple of words to Jeremy. But at the same time I am completely exhausted. Laura and Allie are worn out too. I think even our Energizer Bunny (Caitlin) is feeling a little fatigued. And Beanie fell asleep in the limo tonight as we were chauffeured the short distance from the concert to the hotel.

Today was a loooong day of performing with three other bands in Disneyland. We each took the stage twice, but in between playing we were expected to hang out and sign CDs and schmooze with fans. It was about a hundred degrees with high humidity, and I felt like a melted Popsicle by noon. We didn't leave the park until closing. Exhausting doesn't even begin to describe it.

"Are we sure we really want to go down to Mexico tomorrow?" Allie said as we sat like zombies in the back of the limo.

Laura groaned. "Is that tomorrow? I thought we had tomorrow off."

"According to the schedule, we did," said Allie.

"But you guys said it was okay," Caitlin said in an apologetic voice. "I never would've promised we'd come otherwise."

"It's okay," I reassured her. "It's for a good cause."

"Do you know how cool this is going to be for the orphanage kids?" she said.

"Yeah," said Allie. "What a thrill to see three half-dead girls crawling up on the stage."

"I'll bet it's hot down there," said Laura.

"At least we're almost done with the summer tour," I said, hoping to sound encouraging.

"I feel like I'm done right now," Allie said as she examined the fresh sunburn on her shoulders. "Well done, that is."

STRENGTHEN US

Lord, give us strength

and give us rest

we need Your help

to do our best

please, shine through us

when we feel dull

when we feel empty

please, fill us full

when we're weak

You make us strong

we need Your strength

to get along

we need Your power
poured from above
rain down a shower
of grace and love
amen

Monday, August 29

I really didn't think I'd be saying this, but our concert last night at the orphanage was totally amazing. Not because we were so awesome. Frankly, I think we were only mediocre, if that. Although we were really giving it our best effort under our totally exhausted and overheated circumstances (it was 112 down there!). But the awesome part of the whole evening was the excitement and enthusiasm of everyone at the concert. There were people of all ages, babies and grown-ups and teens and grandmas, and even though I'm sure most of them didn't understand most of what we were singing, their response was so genuine and appreciative. I think it actually refreshed us by the time it was over.

Naturally, we didn't sell any CDs—oh, maybe a couple. But we decided to donate some to the teen center and some to the children's group homes when we took a tour of the complex this morning. We'd arrived just in time for the concert last night and hadn't had time to look around. But what we saw today was pretty impressive. There are a lot of really good people here who've worked hard to make this place what it is today. Even though Caitlin had warned us, I felt stunned at the poverty we saw. I mean, I thought the homeless people in the U.S. were bad off, but they've got it easy compared to the people down here. However, we did manage to raise a little money for their cause with our concert last night, although the tickets were pretty cheap and a lot of people were admitted for free.

But it was kind of fun doing a concert like this. It sort of reminded me of the old days. I mean, there was no fancy lighting or sound systems. No security guards or anything. For a minute I thought we were those three young girls just trying to make our way into the music world again, and it was kind of cool. Well, actually it was hotter than—well, you get the picture. I've never sweated so much in my life.

Let me tell you, we were so thankful to have our bus to return to after the concert. Rosy had kept the generator running and the air conditioner turned on high. And we all just sort of melted into the furniture. Fortunately, Caitlin had her wits about her, and she encouraged us to drink and eat good stuff and then finally got us all off to bed. Just like a little mother.

And to my surprise, I didn't feel totally wiped

when I got up this morning. The plan was to meet
Josh and have breakfast with him and some of the
other staff people, then take a quick tour of the
facility before we hit the road to make our next
gig.

"You guys were fantastic last night," he told
us as soon as he got us seated at a corner table in
the dining room.

I kind of frowned. "Well, the crowd was pretty
fantastic, but we were a little wrung out."

"Hey, everyone here appreciated it a lot."

We visited with Josh while eating a somewhat
unusual breakfast of eggs, beans, and rice.

"This is pretty typical down here," said Josh.
"We eat a lot of beans and rice."

"Yeah," said Caitlin. "I actually put on weight
the last time I was down here."

Josh smiled at her. "Not that anyone would
notice."

Before long people began coming up and asking for introductions to Allie, Laura, and me, and
then we were signing autographs. Rosy and Willy
excused themselves to take care of business,
although I wonder if they were just going back to
the RVs to cool off since it was already ninety
degrees and rising. Then Beanie said she was
going to visit some old friends in the day care
center, and finally Josh said that it was time to
take our tour of the facilities.

"I hope you don't mind that I asked my buddy Mike to drive you girls around," he said to Allie, Laura, and me. "Since my Jeep only has room for three passengers."

"That's fine," I assured him. "I'm sure Caitlin's seen everything anyway." I suspected he wanted some alone time to hang with Caitlin. And she seemed perfectly comfortable with this, so the three of us took off with Mike.

The tour took about an hour, and we three girls decided that we'd like to come back and do another benefit concert and even hang out for a day or two next year—hopefully during the winter when it's cooler. We'll have to discuss this with Willy.

Then Mike dropped us off at the bus, and it was time to go.

"Is Caitlin here?" Rosy called as she did the final preparations to leave.

"Isn't she back yet?" I asked.

"I haven't seen her."

So I looked around the bus, and Rosy was right—Caitlin hadn't come back yet. I went out to check with Willy. "Have you seen Caitlin?"

He shook his head, then looked at his watch. "You girls need to be on the road now. Why don't you tell Rosy to go ahead and take off, and I'll wait here for Caitlin. Do you have any idea where she went?"

"Last I saw, she was with Josh."

Willy grinned. "Well, that probably explains everything. You girls get going and I'll call you if there's a problem. Otherwise, we'll just meet up in Sacramento."

So we're on our way to Sacramento without Caitlin. I'm sure she's perfectly fine, but it's pretty funny that little Ms. Responsible missed the bus. We can't wait to give her a bad time about it.

Tuesday, August 30

Well, Caitlin and Willy made it to Sacramento just fine. She actually only missed the bus by ten minutes. But then ten minutes is ten minutes, and apparently the Redemption bus waits for no one. As it was we didn't get to Sacramento until after midnight. By then we were zonked and pretty much fell into bed because we had to get up early enough to do a concert with Iron Cross at one o'clock the following day—actually the same day.

I barely exchanged a "Hey" with Jeremy before it was time for us to open. And then even afterwards our paths never crossed. I wasn't sure if this was Jeremy's plan or just the way it was. But I suppose I felt a little bummed. Or maybe I was just tired. Everyone seems pretty tired. Allie in particular is dragging. This seems especially odd considering how she is usually bouncing off the walls no matter how hard we've been working. But she's not herself, and she has these dark circles under her eyes that are making everyone nervous.

"Allie, I want you to call your mom," Caitlin said as we were finishing up signing CDs. "Tell her what's up and at the very least have her make a doctor appointment for when we get home next week."

"I'm just tired," complained Allie. "Everyone's tired."

"Well, we're all going back to the hotel," said Caitlin. "And everyone's going to take a nice long nap."

No protests there.

Thursday, September 1

Another concert tonight. This time we were head-lining with a new warm-up band called Wooden Head. It's a guys' band from Sacramento, so you'd think they'd be fairly well received (you know, the home field advantage), but the crowd was only so-so about them. I'll admit I didn't think they were the greatest either, but then everyone's style is different. Plus it's still pretty hot down here, and it was an outdoor concert, so I figured maybe everyone was just so baked that they weren't really responding to the music anyway. Not exactly a happy thought since we were on next. But fortunately the crowd seemed happier when we got onstage, and all in all it wasn't such a bad concert. Although I still felt we were lagging. I mentioned it to Willy afterward.

"It's okay, Chloe. You can't expect to be in top form every night. The whole tour thing just wears on you. Some bands would be a complete mess by now. And this heat doesn't help a bit."

"I'll be glad when it's over, Willy."

He patted my head. "We all will. Only two more concerts and we can go home."

"Home..." I thought about this. I don't think I've ever longed for home as much as I did tonight. Even now, in the "comfort" of this hotel room, I wish I could be like Dorothy and just click my heels together three times and end up in my own bed in my own room at home. Two more concerts.

Saturday, September 3

We performed with Iron Cross tonight. And considering how wiped we all are (even Iron Cross admits to being frazzled), we did okay. But that was all. Just okay. Sometimes I wonder if the audience is ever disappointed in us. Like maybe they're thinking they didn't get their money's worth this time. And I'll admit this bothers me quite a bit, but on the other hand, I don't think there's much we can do about it. The old "you can't squeeze blood from a turnip" saying comes to mind. They could pressure and grind on us, but I seriously doubt we could play any better no matter how hard we tried. We are all just plain tired.

I feel a little bad that I've been mostly ignoring my e-mail lately. I have about a hundred unanswered pieces, and these are from people I actually know—friends and relatives. Although I think about half of these are from Tiffany Knight. I almost cringe every time I see her name in the "from" box. And I control myself from deleting her posts unread. That would be incredibly rude. But really, that girl needs to get a life! I do, however, try to answer the ones from my parents. But that's the best I can do at the moment. I'll catch up with everything next week when we go home. Home. Ahh, just the sound of that word makes me feel better.

HOME

my own sweet home

a peaceful place

where i can rest

in my own space

home is the perfect

spot to be

to just relax
and just be me
it is the place
to show the way
of how my home
will change someday
my Father's home
a place of love
where i will live
far up above
cm

Twenty-Two

Sunday, September 4

We were all hanging in the hotel today, mostly reading, napping, and eating what Caitlin determines is "healthy" food. We're basically trying to recuperate enough to do our final concert tomorrow. It's a biggie with six bands playing all day. Iron Cross will be there, of course, to finish the whole thing off. We're supposed to play before them. Willy says they're saving the best two bands for last. That's pretty cool. And we really wanted to be in top form for this concert.

But then something happened that just knocked us all flat. Mostly me, I think. I'm still feeling pretty horrible about it. And guilty. And sick.

The phone rang about two o'clock in the afternoon. I answered.

"Chloe?"

"Dad?"

"How you doing, honey?"

"Pretty much spent. How about you guys?" Now I always get a little nervous when the parents call, since we tend to e-mail more than use the phone. I start thinking something is wrong, like with Mom or Josh or Caleb. And today was no different, and actually I thought I heard something in his voice.

"Well, something sad happened here in town last night. I think you were friends with Tiffany Knight."

"Yeah. What happened?"

"Tiffany was riding a motorcycle with her dad last night, and they hit gravel, and, well, Tiffany was killed."

"Tiffany was killed?" Allie and Laura were coming over to where I was standing now, their faces concerned.

"Yes, it was a bad wreck. The bike slammed into a telephone pole and the father is in critical condition, but the news said Tiffany died instantly. I wasn't sure if I should call and tell you or not, but then I thought you should know."

"She's dead?"

"I'm sorry, pumpkin."

"I feel horrible."

"I know. It's hard to hear about something like this."

The line was quiet for a few moments, and Allie and Laura were both tugging on me, wanting more information. Finally I said, "Thanks, Dad. I need to tell Allie and Laura about this."

"Chloe?"

"Huh?"

"I love you, honey. And I'm so glad you'll be home soon."

"I love you too, Dad. Tell Mom I love her too. I'll call you back later, okay?"

"Good. That'd be good."

I hung up the phone and turned to Allie and Laura, then noticed that Beanie and Caitlin were looking at me too.

"Tiffany Knight was killed in a motorcycle wreck last night." I know my voice sounded flat and emotionless, but that is not how I felt.

Allie's eyes grew wide. "No way. Tiffany Knight is dead?"

I nodded.

Laura sank into the couch. "Wow. That is so sad."

"Was she a close friend?" asked Beanie.

We all looked at each other, then finally I spoke, trying to sound normal over the huge lump that had lodged itself in my throat. "Actually, she was trying to be my friend," I admitted. "But I spent most of my time just blowing her off."

"That's not true," said Laura. "You were always nice to her."

"That's right," agreed Allie. "You were probably nicer to her than anyone else at school."

I shook my head. "No, I wasn't." And then I began to sob. I couldn't even talk anymore. Everyone tried to comfort me, but it was useless.

Finally, I just had to come into the bedroom. I told them I wanted to take a nap. But I cannot sleep.

I feel like the most rotten human being on the planet. I can remember, in vivid detail, every single time I resented Tiffany, tried to avoid her, wanted to escape her—every single miserable thing. And I make myself sick. I even glanced back through my diary to see if it was true. And there I am whining and complaining about how God has given me this "hard challenge to love Tiffany." What is wrong with me? I am such a hopeless, pathetic loser.

And I'm sure God must be ashamed of me down to His shoes. I don't think I've ever felt such self-loathing in my life. Or at least not since I became a Christian. I don't see how I'll be able to perform tomorrow. How can I stand up there on the stage and tell everyone to love others the way Jesus loves them when I am such a total hypocrite?

NO WAY OUT
i ache
with grief
find no
relief
my heart's

in pain
i feel
insane
with guilt
and doubt
i want
to shout
take me
instead
wish i
were dead
wish i'd
known then
or that
i'd been
a better
friend
before
the end
i ache
with grief
find no
relief
and
no
way
out
cm

Twenty-Three

Monday, September 5

I know Allie and Laura were seriously worried about me before today's concert. I tried to act as if I was going to be okay, but inside I felt like someone had put my guts in the blender and just whirled them for about an hour. Still, I thought I was keeping up a brave front.

"I heard about your friend," said Jeremy.

I'd purposely sat by myself in a quiet area of the large room set up for musicians to eat and rest between performances. I thought I was doing a pretty good job of pretending to read my Bible, with my knees pulled up to my chin, sending out a strong "do not disturb this spiritual person" message. But the truth was, I was just sitting there like a vegetable, tucked into the corner of the sofa in this miserable little heap of guilt and grief. But I was surprised to see Jeremy there since he usually avoids this scene. I'd only gone there myself because I thought I could be ignored amid all the noise and busyness.

"Mind if I join you?"

I shrugged. "I'm not very good company."

"I know."

We sat there in silence for a good five minutes before Jeremy spoke. "I'm not going to say I know how you feel, Chloe. But I think there must be a reason you're taking this so hard. You want to talk about it?"

"Did the girls send you to rescue me?"

He smiled. "Sort of. They're worried about you. They said you're taking this too hard."

"Too hard?" I felt slightly angry now. "You know why I feel like crud? It's because this girl who died, Tiffany Knight, had been trying and trying to be my friend, and I couldn't stand her. I mean, I tried and I tried to love her, but she just basically made me crazy."

"Laura told me about how she used to beat you up."

"Jesus was beaten," I tossed back. "But He loved His enemies."

"You're not Jesus, Chloe."

I sighed.

"And Allie said that no one liked this girl. And that you were nicer to her than anyone—"

"But that wasn't good enough," I said, fresh tears filling my eyes. "She'd been e-mailing me a lot recently, and I never even read her e-mails—not a single one. I mean, if I'd known this was going to happen, I would've read them, Jeremy—I would've written back. I would've told her to give her heart to God and—" Then I totally lost it. And despite our pact, Jeremy put his arms around me and held me for a while. But it was a brotherly sort of hug. I absolutely knew this, and I really don't think it was wrong. Finally I was able to stop crying. I sat back and blew my nose on the red bandanna that he pulled from his pocket.

"So, you're worried that she died without giving her heart to God?"

I nodded as I held his bandanna out to him.

He smiled. "Keep it."

"The last time I talked to her about God, she admitted that she was still trying to figure it out."

"Then maybe she did."

I frowned. "You didn't know this girl, Jeremy. I hate to say it, especially since she's—she's dead, but she was the shallowest person I've ever known in my life." I started crying again. But not so hard this time. Still, I felt like the scum of the earth for saying what I'd just said. I used his bandanna to blot my eyes and tried to explain myself better. "I feel totally rotten for not reaching out to Tiffany more, for not loving her better. And now it's too late."

"Chloe," Jeremy said in a quiet but intense voice, as if to really get my attention.

I looked up at him.

"Listen to me, okay?"

I nodded.

"Do you trust God with everything, every part of your life? Do you think He's big enough to handle it?"

"Of course."

"Then you need to trust Him with this. Do you really think what happened to Tiffany Knight was totally out of God's control?"

"I'm not sure."

"Was Tiffany a part of your life? I mean, did you share Jesus with her and pray for her and stuff like that?"

"Yeah. I did. A lot."

"So, she was part of your life?"

"Yeah."

"Do you really think God wasn't involved with what happened to her? Do you think He'd allow her to die without getting it squared away with Him first?"

"I don't know."

"Maybe you need to just trust Him with this."

I nodded. "Yeah. I suppose I haven't been doing that."

"And you need to ask Him to forgive you."

"I did."

"Then you need to forgive yourself."

"I know you're right, but it's hard."

"When we don't forgive ourselves, it's like spitting on Jesus, Chloe."

I knew what he was saying. I think I've said as

much to other people before. "I know. I know..."

"Do you want to pray about it?"

I nodded.

And there in the midst of all these other musicians, we bowed our heads and began to pray. But then something amazing began to happen. I heard others walking over to us, and pretty soon there was a circle of about a dozen people sitting and standing all around us in this circle. They were putting their hands on my shoulders and head and actually praying for me too. It was incredible. When we finally finished, I was crying again. But these felt like healing tears. I thanked everyone. And we hugged and it was like the body of Christ in action. Amazing.

So just before it was time for Redemption to perform, Laura said, "Maybe we should just skip the rock-paper-scissors routine tonight. Allie or I can speak."

I shook my head. "No, I want to, if you guys don't mind."

"You sure?" Allie's eyes were still full of concern.

I nodded.

So we went out and played. I think it was the best we'd played in days, maybe even weeks. And finally it was time to share, and I silently prayed that God would somehow sift through all my emotions and help me say what it was I wanted to say.

"A friend of ours died Saturday," I began, and the crowd grew instantly quiet. "Her name was Tiffany Knight and she was seventeen and about to start her junior year. She was killed instantly in a motorcycle wreck, and her dad is in critical condition right now. In fact, let's all take a moment of silence to think of Tiffany and to pray for Mr. Knight." I bowed my head and blinked back the tears that were filling my eyes again, and after a moment I continued.

"I want to admit something to you guys tonight. I knew that God had called me to love Tiffany Knight, but the truth was, I found it really hard to love this girl. She had beaten me up when I was a freshman, and she made fun of people who were overweight or unattractive or just different. To be perfectly honest, Tiffany Knight was pretty obnoxious.

"But about a year ago, she had decided she wanted to become good friends with me. She started e-mailing me when we were on tour, and then she'd follow me around while we were at school. And I didn't always like that. Still, I knew without a doubt that God had called me to love Tiffany. And I tried. I really did. Again and again I tried. But I think I mostly failed.

"I used to believe that God had given me Tiffany Knight as my personal cross to bear—you know what I mean? That hard thing in your life that just never seems to go away? I honestly thought I would have to drag this girl around with me for the rest of my days. But now she's dead. And you know what? I wish, more than anything, that she were alive and that I could take her everywhere with me. I wish that I could be her best friend and love her the way Jesus loves me, and I wish I could talk to her and pray with her and all sorts of things. But guess what? It's too late. She's dead. I'll never have the chance again."

Tears were running down my cheeks now. "And this is what I want to say to you. Everybody has a Tiffany Knight in their lives. Or maybe you are one yourself. I'm talking about that guy who hasn't accepted Jesus as his Savior, that girl who still thinks that God doesn't care about her. And what I want to tell you all tonight is that we don't know how long these people are going to be around. I'm sure Tiffany didn't get up Saturday morning and realize that she was about to live the last day of her life. So my challenge to everyone, including myself, is this: Let's live each day as if it were our last, let's love everyone like we won't be seeing them again. Let's live our lives for God so that we'll have no regrets when it's time to call it a day."

I looked out over the crowd then held up my fist and shouted, "No regrets!" And everyone else did the same. Then I said, "I want to dedicate our next and final song to Tiffany Knight. Tiffany, if you can hear us, this one is for you."

And then we sang "The Heaven Song." After we were done, Iron Cross came up, but before they started singing, Jeremy began to speak, picking up where I'd left off, almost as if it had been planned, which it hadn't. He gave a powerful invitation for them to follow Jesus or to recommit their lives, and almost everybody raised their hands. Then he led them in a beautiful prayer.

I have decided that God wastes nothing. Not even what seems like a perfectly senseless death of a life that was never fully lived. And although I'm still sad and sobered, I am trusting God for all this. It's all I can do at the moment.

THE HEAVEN SONG
there's something in the air
that washed away my care
like a shower of spring rain
erasing all my pain
God's breath breathing down on me
filling me with energy
washing me with joy and peace
giving me this sweet release
i can walk or i can fly
like an eagle through the sky
or enjoy a happy ride

zipping down a rainbow slide
God's breath breathing down on me
filling me with energy
washing me with joy and peace
giving me this sweet release
i can sing and i can dance
i can make the horses prance
i can play games with baboons
or i can walk upon the moon
God's breath breathing down on me
filling me with energy
washing me with joy and peace
giving me this sweet release
i can swim beneath the sea
seeing wonders that see me
i can build a house of gold
or listen to the songs of old
God's breath breathing down on me
filling me with energy
washing me with joy and peace
giving me this sweet release
i can do most anything
bow before the King of kings
i can thank Him for His grace
and praise Him for this heavenly place

cm

Twenty-Four

Tuesday, September 6

After the concert last night, I decided to read Tiffany's e-mails. Everyone had pretty much gone to bed and I was sitting in the living area of our suite, just quietly reading on my laptop. The first two posts were fairly typical. She was telling me about what she'd been doing this summer, and it sounded pretty uneventful to me. "Too bad," I was thinking.

Then I came to the third post, and she was really talking about God a lot and about some of the things she had heard at church that day. Then by the fourth post, I could tell that God was really at work in her, and by the fifth one, she had actually gotten down on her knees and given her heart to God. Well, by then I was probably jumping up and down and yelling. At least that's what everyone told me when I woke them up.

"What's the matter?" Laura demanded as she rubbed her eyes.

"Yeah, what's up?" said Allie.

"I'm reading Tiffany's e-mail," I told them.

"What's it say?" Caitlin asked as everyone began to gather around with interest.

"Okay, you guys, listen to this! It's the fifth e-mail Tiffany sent me this summer, written in late July:

I really did it, Chloe. You may not believe me, but I totally did it. Tonight, after church got out, I was thinking about the sermon and I realized that I am just like that blind man he was talking about. And just like that blind man, I need Jesus to open my eyes. But the only way I can get Him to open my eyes is to open my heart. So, believe it or not, I got down on my knees tonight, right here in my own bed-room, and I asked Jesus to come into my heart. I stayed there waiting for what seemed a pretty long time, and I didn't really feel any different. I guess I sort of wondered why it wasn't working when kazam, it felt just like electricity run-ning through me. Now, I gotta ask you, is that normal? Did you feel like you just got zapped when you invited Jesus into your heart, or am I just special, or maybe even weird? I really need to know. Love, Tiffany."

"And you never wrote her back?" said Allie. "I never even read these e-mails until tonight," I reminded her. I'd already tried to explain my little guilt trip over this to them, but apparently Allie wasn't quite awake yet.

"Are there more?" asked Caitlin.

"Yeah, there's a bunch more."

And so I continued to read. And to everyone's great relief, Tiffany's electrical jolt did prove to be the real thing, and she did believe she had given her heart to Jesus.

"Listen to this," I told them.

"I had to forgive someone today, Chloe. So far I've only told God and now you. But back when I was a little kid and my mom was married to Jeff, my stepdad at the time, well, he did things to me that he shouldn't have done. It's hard to say the words out loud, but I think I can write them. Jeff sexually abused me. He did it quite a few times too. He always bought me a toy or ice cream afterward and told me that if I told anyone I'd get into really big trouble. And so I never did. Even after my mom divorced him, I never forgot. It's one of those creepy things that goes with you every single day of your life. It messes with your mind, Chloe. I don't know how else to explain it. And I think it messed me up good.

But tonight I realized, after reading
my new Bible, that I have to forgive Jeff.
And so I asked God to help me. And I think
that I've done it. But I do have a question:
Do I have to like him now? Because I still
really don't like him. And if I saw him
today, I'd probably feel pretty cruddy.
Does that mean I didn't really forgive
him? Do I have to forgive him again?

Oh, man, I have so many questions,
Chloe. And so far you haven't even written
back. Oh well, I suppose you're pretty
busy doing all those concerts and everything. I keep thinking I'm going to get
tickets and come to one of them, but then I
have this stupid job at the pizza place at
the mall, and well, I'm not very good at
saving up money. But maybe I'll get to do it
one of these days. Until then. Love,
Tiffany."

"Wow," said Beanie. "That's amazing. It seems
like God was really working on that girl's heart."

"I feel so bad that I never read these," I said.
"I wish I could've written back."

"What's the next one say?" asked Allie eagerly.

Well, it was already after two in the morning,
but I knew I wasn't going to bed anytime soon. And
so I read another.

"This is dated August 15," I told them.

"Hey Chloe, it looks like you're never going to answer my e-mail, are you? I saw your mom at the mall today, and I asked her if you had been abducted or some-thing. Just kidding. But I told her I hadn't heard from you, and she said that you were super-duper busy and didn't even have time to talk to your own parents very much. So I've forgiven you for not answering me. And you know what else? I've decided that I'm going to just keep writing you anyway. I don't care if you ever read any of these letters. You know why? Because it's sort of good for me to write them. It's kind of like therapy, you know? And after I get done I always feel better."

I paused then. "That's sort of like how I feel about my diary."

"Keep reading," urged Allie.

"Anyway I was reading in my Bible today, the part about loving my enemies, and there's this really mean girl where I work who acts like she totally hates my guts. I swear she's trying to get me fired. And one day she stole my tips. Anyway, it hits me like—boom, a flash of lightning—I need to love this chick. Her name is Frannie Campbell and she's kind of chubby and homely and smells like onions and fish. But I've decided if that's really what God wants, I will try to love her. But let me tell you, she is one unlovable lady. Also, I want you to know that I am praying for you and your band now. I hope you're okay and having a great time being famous. Love, Tiffany."

"She's a crack-up," said Beanie. "I think I would've liked this girl."

"Well, she wasn't always like that," said Laura.

"Maybe she was starting to change," said Allie.

"Or maybe she _was_ like that," I said, "but we were just too busy to notice."

"Are there any more?" asked Caitlin.

"Just two," I told them. So I read the next one, and it was more about Frannie and how she could get really gross when she had gas, which actually made us all laugh pretty hard. Then finally the last one, dated September 2, the day before the accident.

"Dear Chloe, I hope everything's going really great for you and your band. Your mom told me that you guys will be back in school next week, and I can't wait to see you in person and tell you everything that's been happening in my life. I'll bet you won't even believe me. I had the day off today. I think it was a scheduling mistake since the mall is busier than ever with back-to-school shoppers. Just the same, I was really glad not to have to go to work. And at first I thought maybe I'd head over to the mall to do some back-to-school shopping for myself, then I decided, nah, I'd rather just hang out around home.

"And you know what? My dad, I mean my real dad, showed up totally unexpected on this amazing Harley that he'd recently bought from a friend. He was visiting his parents, but he came over and took me for a ride on his new hog. I wanted to ask him how much it cost since he's been a little lazy about child support lately, but then I realized that maybe that would be rude. So instead I decided to just enjoy hanging with him since I hadn't seen him for like five years.

"Anyway, we rode out to the lake and just sat and talked for a while. And I told him about how I'd invited Jesus into my heart and how it was changing my life and how I was so much happier—you know, all that good stuff. Oh, he tried to be nice about it, but he just didn't get it. So I told him it wasn't all that long ago that my good friend Chloe Miller (famous girl rock star) was telling me these exact same things and I didn't get them either. 'Don't worry, Dad,' I told him. 'When God is ready and you are ready, you'll get it then.' And I really think he will. Just like you couldn't push me into God's arms, I know I can't push my dad either. But I'm praying for him. Because I know he's one unhappy dude. Mostly he just complained about his life to me and how he's made so many stupid mistakes. Well, duh. It's not like I don't know. I mean, it was his stupid mistakes that got me all messed up by Jeff my step-dad. But I didn't tell him any of this. I figure there's only so much a person can handle at one time.

"Anyway, he's coming over tomorrow and we're going to take a day trip up into the hills and maybe even go fishing. Weird. Can you imagine a girl like me, who doesn't like to mess her nails or hair, actually going fishing??? Well, I am changing, Chloe. Just you wait and see! Love always, Tiffany."

Okay, now I was crying again. But they weren't the miserable tears of guilt and grief and confusion. They were a mix of happy tears and regret that I hadn't taken the time to answer these e-mails and gotten to know Tiffany better. I looked up from my computer to see that everyone in the room was crying too. Soon we were all hugging, and finally we sat down and just prayed. We prayed for both of Tiffany's parents, and very specifically, her dad. And we prayed for a lot of things, and finally it was almost five in the morning.

"Maybe we should get some sleep," said Caitlin. "Since we're heading out at eight."

So we got about two hours' sleep before we loaded our stuff and our tired selves into the bus. Then we mostly slept off and on throughout the day until Rosy finally pulled into our hometown around midnight tonight. It was so great being met by my dad, loaded into his car, and driven home, where I am about to go to sleep in my very own bed again. Yes, I am totally worn out and weary, but ever so thankful to be home again.

HOME AT LAST
i want to tiptoe
through my house
take it all in
like a mouse
to smell the smells
breathe the air
to hear the squeak
on the top stair
to feel the rug
'neath my feet
to hear the clock
tick so sweet
to see the window
in my room
where i have stood
to watch the moon
to feel the softness
of my bed
to feel my pillow
'neath my head
cm

Twenty-Five

Wednesday, September 7

I called my mom at her work yesterday morning while we were on the road and asked if she'd contact Tiffany's mom to let her know our band would like to play a song or two for the memorial service if that was all right with Tiffany's family. Mom promised me she would let them know. As it turned out, Tiffany's mom was really touched and said that Tiffany would've really liked that.

And so it was that we found ourselves performing on our first day back home. Even though we were tired, we didn't mind. First we played a song that Tiffany had always told me was her favorite. Then we played "The Heaven Song."

The church was packed full. I was surprised to see so many kids from school there, but I overheard Bethany Crandall in the bathroom, saying that the school had given the rest of the day off to any kids attending. And since the funeral was over by two o'clock, they must've figured that earned them about an hour's worth of free time. Although I'd like to believe that some of the kids were actually there for Tiffany's sake. I know that I was. So were Allie and Laura and Jake and Cesar and

Marty and a bunch of other Christian kids.

Caitlin and Beanie had even considered coming, although they didn't know Tiffany, but then decided they'd better head off to school. It was a wet and sloppy farewell last night. But in some ways, I think we were all ready to see the summer end and get back to a life that feels a little more normal, although I'm wondering if I even know what normal really is.

After we sang "The Heaven Song," Tiffany's mom asked me if I would say a few words about Tiffany. This was pretty much out of the blue, and at first I was uncertain about it, but now I'm glad I had the opportunity.

"Tiffany and I didn't exactly start out as friends," I began, and I could see some eyes lighting up as if they suddenly remembered our "little" problems during the beginning of our freshman year. "But we both grew up some, and during the past year we mended our fences. Tiffany proved to me that she could be a very loyal friend. Unfortunately, my life with the band and the concert tour didn't give me much time to return the friendship. And I guess I feel pretty bad about that now. You see, she'd sent me a bunch of e-mails while I was on tour, but I never had time to read them—not until she died, that is. But as I read them I realized how she needed me to be her friend."

I paused now and looked out over the crowd of mostly young faces. Okay, I'll admit it. I did want to make them feel uncomfortable today. I wanted them to experience a tiny bit of the guilt that I'd been buried under when I first heard of her death. Why did I want to do this? Not to torture or torment anyone, but just to remind them of what's important.

"Doesn't EVERYONE need a friend?" I asked. "I mean, whether a person is obnoxious or introverted or obese or anorexic or paranoid or self-centered or preppy or grungy or freaky or geeky or just plain average, don't we ALL need a friend?" I saw some heads nodding, and even some moist eyes. "And I realized, as Tiffany opened up even more to me in her e-mails and told me a little about her life, that it hadn't been so easy for her, and that she was pretty lonely. It was pretty obvious that she really needed a friend. And then I felt even worse. But then I continued to read until I came to some of her most recent e-mails, and that's when I discovered that she had found the perfect friend. Like Pastor Fitzgerald said, Tiffany had given her heart to Jesus. And I could tell by the way she wrote in her e-mails that it was for real. I could tell that Tiffany was a changed person. I really liked the person she was becoming, and if she hadn't died in that motorcycle wreck last weekend, I feel certain that she and I would've become really good friends this year."

I felt tears going down my cheeks now, but I just let them run. "Even though I know Tiffany is in heaven now—and believe me, I have no doubts about that—I feel sad that I won't get to see our friendship grow down here on earth. It's like we'd been through all the hard stuff together, and it was just about to get good, but now she's gone." I took a breath. "And I am really going to miss her."

Then I looked at the crowd again, pausing to scan the familiar faces, some now blotchy and streaked with tears. "But at least I know I'm going to see her again when we meet up in heaven. And let me tell you, there's going to be an outrageous celebration going on up there on that homecoming day. I just hope that everyone here today will be there too. And I have a feeling Tiffany would agree with me on that. I have a feeling she's up there right now saying, 'Hey, you guys, wake up and smell the coffee. Figure out who God really is and what your life is all about. Get it together before it's too late.'" I paused again, unsure of how to end my little mini sermon. "Well, I guess that's all I have to say."

The pastor smiled at me as he returned to the pulpit. And picking up where I'd left off, he gave an invitation to everyone in the church to surrender their lives to Jesus. I kept my head down as he invited people to raise their hands. I prayed that God would nudge their hearts and that they would respond, and according to Jake (who admitted he'd peeked), that happened.

Allie and Laura and I stayed and visited briefly, but I think we were all pretty wiped out. Allie had a doctor's appointment since she seems to have some sort of bug, so we slipped out the back door while people were still visiting.

I plan to visit Tiffany's gravesite later on. Right now all I want to do is sleep until Christmas.

LATER
see ya later
Tiffany
beyond the sky
beyond the sea
see you in the
land above
land of peace
land of love
see ya later
Tiffany
thank you for
forgiving me
sing and dance
and have no care
when i'm done
i'll meet you there
cm

Wednesday, September 14

Well, guess I didn't really need to sleep until Christmas after all. But I did sleep for a couple of days. It turns out that Allie has mono. That's why she was dragging so much at the end of the tour. So now she's supposed to get a lot of rest and consequently hasn't even been to school yet. She told me that the doctor said she may not be able to go to school for FOUR whole weeks.

"How'd you get mono anyway?" I asked when I went to visit her last weekend. "Isn't it supposed to be from kissing or something?"

She didn't say anything.

"Allie? Did you and Brett kiss during the tour?"

She still didn't say anything.

"Allie!"

She made a face at me and turned to look out the window of her new bedroom. Oh yeah, I should mention that Allie gave Elise enough money to put a down payment on a house, which Elise and Davie moved into shortly before our tour ended. It's in a new development at the edge of town, and although it wasn't an expensive house, it's a whole lot nicer and bigger than their old apartment. I guess they plan to live there even after Elise and Willy get married in December, since Willy's place is pretty small.

"Did you come here just to make me more miserable?" demanded Allie.

I shook my head. "I'm sorry. But I am curious. Did you and Brett ever kiss?"

She made a face. "Only a couple of times."

"Do you think—?"

"Oh, I don't know what to think, Chloe. Are you going to suggest that Brett gave me mono, that he goes around kissing every girl in sight and picked up some bug and...?"

"Well, it could happen. Have you asked him?"

"Nooo."

"What about our pact, Allie?"

She shrugged. "It didn't stop you."

"Yeah. I guess you're right. But we only did it once, Al. And we were both really sorry, and I'm pretty certain it won't happen again."

"At least not while we're stuck here at home."

"Huh?"

"Well, the doctor said I might not be ready to go on tour again for months."

"Months?"

She nodded.

"Months? Seriously."

"I'm sorry, Chloe." She looked close to tears now.

"It's not really your fault, Allie. If anything, I should be the one to get mono. I deserve it."

She laughed. "No, you don't. No one deserves it."

"Yeah, I guess."

"But I'm messing everything up for everyone."

"No, you're not." Suddenly, I remembered what Jeremy had said about trusting God for every-thing when Tiffany died. "We're just going to have to trust God with this whole thing. If we're sup-posed to go on tour again this year, then you'll be well enough to go. If not, we'll wait until you are."

"Willy already let Omega know. He said they weren't even that surprised. I guess stuff like this happens a lot in the music circuit. He said that since we did such a great job on tour this summer and both our CDs are still selling well, then maybe we just all need a good-sized break anyway."

I sighed. "You know what, Allie? I feel kind of relieved. This summer really wiped me out. I mean, I've only written a couple of songs since last spring. Maybe we need a hiatus."

"What's that?"

"A break, you know."

"Oh, yeah."

"Have you told Laura yet?"

"No, I thought I should tell you first."

"Well, she might be relieved too. You know

she's started her classes at community college this week, but she figured she might have to drop them when we went back on tour."

"Maybe she won't."

"Are you sad that you don't get to come to school?"

She nodded. "I never thought I'd say it, but I am. I was looking forward to seeing our friends again...to getting back to the old life."

"Just take care of yourself," I told her. "Do everything the doctor says and maybe you can come back to school sooner."

"I hope so."

"Guess this means no practicing too."

She nodded glumly. "Sorry."

"No, Allie, don't keep saying 'sorry.' It's not your fault. And like I said, God's in control. We have to trust Him in this. He must want us to have this break for a reason. Life goes on, you know. Whether we're touring the country or back here at home, life goes on. And it's going to be okay."

I think she felt a little better when I left. And I totally meant what I said. I do want to learn to trust God in everything. Whether I'm onstage being encored by an ecstatic crowd, or doing my detested math homework by myself in my room, I want to trust God and just be where He wants me to be—and be happy about it.

FACE THE MUSIC
getting up
each new day
ready to live
life God's way
face the music
that's how it goes
what comes next
nobody knows
whether it's fast
or super slow
whether you stay
or go, go, go
face the music
that's how it goes
what comes next
nobody knows
whether you're sick
or feeling great
whether it's early
or getting late
face the music
that's how it goes
what comes next
nobody knows
just live each day
and do your best
and in the end
you'll be blessed

face the music
that's how it goes
what comes next
nobody knows
cm

Twenty-Six

Friday, September 16

Willy and Elise are so cute these days. They've been happily planning their wedding, and subsequently their life, but they were so eager to get married that they just decided to hang it all and get married next month. I don't think I can blame them, really. I mean, if you know you're going to marry someone and you believe it's God's will, well, why not just leap in with both feet and figure out all the details later? Of course, that's just me, and I could be wrong. What do I know at the ripe old age of seventeen and a half?

But I was pretty touched when Elise invited Laura and me over for dinner last night and asked us if we'd like to be bridesmaids in her wedding.

"Allie is going to be my maid of honor," she said, smiling at her daughter. "And the truth is, I really don't have many friends—or much of a life, for that matter. And I had such a great time with you girls on that last road trip. It felt like we were all so close. And, well, do you think it would look too ridiculous for a thirty-five-year-old woman to have teenagers as her bridesmaids?"

"I think it's cool," I told her.

"Yeah, me too," said Laura. "It's like we've been this road sort of family already. Why not keep a good thing going?"

"You don't need to give me a shower," said Elise. "Willy and I already have more things than we need."

But we've decided to do something special for Elise. Laura suggested we all pitch in to get them a dining room set since their new dining room is conspicuously empty. And since we can afford it, we might just do that, although I don't have a clue as to where or how you go about doing such a thing. But I figure my mom will have some ideas.

And so it's all settled. Allie, Laura, and I will be Elise's bridesmaids, and hopefully we'll have it together enough by then to play some music at the reception, though this will be dependent on Allie's recovery. So far she seems to be steadily improving. But we've discovered that just because she feels pretty good one day doesn't necessarily mean that she'll feel good the next day. Mostly she just needs to keep resting and taking it easy.

Saturday, September 24

Today was one of those spectacular fall days where the sky is so blue that it almost hurts your eyes, and the leaves are starting to turn colors—glorious. Anyway, I wanted to get outside and enjoy it, so I rode my bike up to the cemetery this morning, just to hang out for a while. Visit my old friends.

Okay, I know that sounds kind of weird, not to mention slightly morbid, but I still like going up there. I like to visit Katherine Lucinda McCall's grave. She's the young woman who died in 1901, and her headstone reads, "May she dance with the angels." I used to spend a lot of time at her grave back when I was fourteen and fifteen and depressed and dark. But Katherine Lucinda was good company back then, back when I had no friends, no life, no God. It was also back then that I finally came across, quite by accident (God's accident, that is), Clay Berringer's grave and was struck by the words of life found there. That's when I first gave my heart to God.

But today, I wanted to visit Tiffany's grave. And I must admit that felt a little strange. I mean, Tiffany was someone I actually knew, talked to, spent time with, and even hated at one time, although I try not to think about that now. I'd stopped by the florist's shop next to the Paradiso and gotten a small bouquet of white roses. I'm not even sure why I picked white roses, but maybe I thought Tiffany would like that. I hadn't been to her grave before, but Cesar had told me where it was, not too far from Clay Berringer's grave, and I found it pretty easily. I put my roses by her headstone, and they actually looked quite nice, kind of sweet and pure. Maybe that's how Tiffany feels now that she's with God in heaven.

I sat on the ground next to her grave and asked God to tell Tiffany "hey" for me and that I'd gotten her e-mails and was happy that she'd finally figured it all out. And then to my surprise I began to cry. At first I wasn't sure why I was crying. I mean, I'd assumed I'd gotten this all over with and out of my system weeks ago. But there I was sitting next to Tiffany Knight's grave and just sobbing like a fool.

"I'm so sorry, Tiffany," I said in a choked-up voice. "I'm sorry I wasn't a better friend to you while you were alive on earth. I'm sorry I judged you, even when I knew that Jesus said not to judge." I went on and on, telling Tiffany how bad I felt and asking her to forgive me. And finally I stopped crying and just sat there with the sun beating down on my head.

Now honestly, I don't know if Tiffany could really hear me or if she even cares about earthly things anymore since I'm sure the glories of heaven are distraction enough. But I guess I just needed to say these things, maybe for my own sake. Besides, I believe that anything's possible with God, and He could send her a message for me if He wanted to. Then, for the second or third time, I asked God to forgive me and help me move on. And then I did something I've never done before, and may never do again. I asked Him to give me some kind of a sign, some sort of assurance, that everything was really okay between me and Tiffany and Him.

Okay, I don't know if this was a real sign from God or not, but it felt like it to me. I opened my eyes and looked up just in time to see a small brown sparrow land right on the bouquet of roses by Tiffany's headstone. The little sparrow just sat there for what must've been a full minute, looking at me, and then it flew away. Just like that.

Well, I thanked God and stood up relieved, thinking how forgiveness is like that. It arrives on the wings of a fragile bird, touches your life, and then moves on. But you feel better because you are made clean and whole and whiter than the roses I got for Tiffany today.

I prayed for Tiffany's dad as I rode my bike home. He's still in the hospital but is expected to make a fairly full recovery. Physically anyway. I'm sure that he's really hurting on the inside. Everyone in our church has been praying for this poor man. And Willy's even gone over to visit him a couple of times. Willy used to be a Harley guy too, and I'm guessing that gives them some common ground. I've been praying for Willy too, that God will use him to reach Tiffany's dad. And I believe it will happen.

SPARROW SONG

mercy comes

on sparrow wings

with a rush

then off it springs

heal me, God

make me new

fill me with

what's good and true

God's touch is

a gentle one

like the breeze

or warmth of sun

heal me, God

make me new

fill me with

what's good and true

cm

Twenty-Seven

Thursday, September 29

Here's weird. For the past two weeks I've been going to school every single day, but Allie and Laura aren't there. It's like after months of eating, sleeping, and hanging together 24/7, they've been sucked right out of my life. I think I've actually been experiencing something akin to culture shock (that's when you move to a completely different place, like from New York to Nepal).

But I'm trying to make the best of it, and I'm trying to reach out to the kids around me. And I've had some really amazing talks with Kim Peterson. It seems that she's really questioning some things since Tiffany Knight died.

"I know it sounds weird to be so affected by this," she told me today, "especially since I basically couldn't stand the girl." She sighed and shook her head sadly. "And I feel pretty bad saying that, but it's the truth. But ever since Tiffany's death I can't help but wonder what happens after we die. And it's really driving me nuts. I have a hard time sleeping and everything. Do you think I'm going crazy, Chloe?"

"Not at all. I think God is just trying to get your attention. And it's a good question, Kim. What DOES happen after we die?"

She just shook her head. "Usually I'm the one with all the answers. I mean, I'm even supposed to be writing this col—" Then she stopped herself suddenly. "Well, anyway, I'm coming up completely blank on this particular question."

So I tried to share with her what I believe as well as what the Bible says about the afterlife, but I can tell she's going to have to mull these things over herself. Even so, I feel hopeful for her. She has one of the most honest and search- ing hearts I've ever seen, and I am positive that God isn't going to let her hang out to dry for too long. But I am curious about what mysterious thing she is writing that has to do with questions and God. Maybe someday she'll tell me. In the meantime, I'm glad that we're friends. But even so, I miss Allie and Laura.

I still see them, of course, but it's not the same—and we're not doing music. It's like my life is turned upside down or inside out or maybe just sideways. At first I thought I was having an identity crisis, like I'm so hooked into being a "celebrity" that I'm unable to adjust to normal life. However, I don't think that's really the case. And even though Laura and Allie are definitely missing from my daily experience, I still enjoy my other friends, and it's been great hooking back up with them again.

However, as much as I love the kids here at school, and I do have a lot of very good friends, I'm seriously worried that I may have outgrown the whole high school experience. Now this isn't something I would go around and announce to the general public, and certainly not to my friends at Harrison High because I'm sure they wouldn't get it at all. I don't even quite get it myself. And it actually bothers me a lot since I'm sure it could appear snooty to some.

But the idea of graduating early is becoming more and more appealing to me, and that's why I met with Mrs. King to discuss this possibility today.

"I hate to say it, Chloe, but it just makes sense for you to move on," she told me. "As much as I'd love to see you around here, I can understand how you must feel after all the incredible life experiences you've had during the last year."

"At first I thought it was great being back here in school. And I was so glad to see my old friends. But after being on tour and, well, everything, I almost feel like I'm going backwards now."

"And you're probably not being terribly challenged academically."

"Maybe in math."

She smiled.

And so it's settled. The paperwork is signed, and I'll be taking some tests and whatnot and we'll see how it goes. But according to Mrs. King, it should be a fairly simple and painless procedure and I'll even be able to march with the graduating class in the spring if I want. Right now, I'm not even sure that I care, but I might by then so I guess I'll keep my options open.

Naturally, Allie was not overly thrilled when I told her my latest news on the phone tonight.

"That's not fair," she said in typical Allie fashion, which in itself is encouraging because I can tell she really must be feeling better.

"Why not?"

"You and Laura are both leaving me behind."

"We're not leaving you anywhere, silly. It just simplifies things for me to be done with high school so that—"

"So that you can run off and marry Jeremy Baxter?" she said in a taunting voice.

I laughed. "Oh yeah, Allie. Like I'm going to get married at seventeen. Give me a break. No, so that I can focus my attention on music and song-writing and maybe even take some college level correspondence courses while we're on the road."

"You really think we'll get to tour again?" she asked in a meek voice.

"Of course. As soon as you're well, that is. And

don't worry, there's no hurry anyway. I'll have a lot to get done in the next month or two, taking tests and stuff."

"And I guess I can keep doing my school work while we're on the road."

"Yeah. And who knows, maybe you could graduate early too, if you worked a little harder."

"Really?"

"You could talk to Mrs. King about it."

"Cool."

"You know it's partly your fault that I decided to do this."

"How's that, Chloe?"

"Well, being at school without you and Laura around has been kind of weird."

"Ya miss me?"

"What d'ya think?"

"I think ya miss me." I could hear the smile in her voice.

"So, keep taking it easy, Al, so you can come back to school sooner."

After I hung up the phone I went out to the practice room and jammed loud and hard for a couple of hours. Man, did that ever feel good. Then I settled down and began to work on a new song that I'd written recently. And it might just be me, but I think it's pretty good too. I think I might be evolving both as a musician and a song-writer—maybe as a person too. Somehow being

back at school with high school-aged kids makes
me realize that I have grown up some.

GROWIN' UP
i used to dress in
Mommy's clothes
high-heeled pumps
and baggy hose
bright red lips
and beads that shone
i would imagine
i was grown
all dressed up
and nowhere to go
why's it take
so long to grow?
then i threw away
my dresses
turned to grunge
and cut my tresses
sporting my
new attitude
darkness was
my new world view
all dressed up
and no place to go
why's it take
so long to grow?
then i tried a

brand-new look
began to live
by God's good book
changin' from
the inside out
seeing what life's
really about
all dressed up
with someplace to go
thank You, God
for making me grow
cm

Saturday, October 22

Willy and Elise got married today. As planned, Allie was the maid of honor and Laura and I were bridesmaids. And although I'm sure some of the older people wondered about this, I was person-ally honored, especially since I've never been in a wedding before. Okay, once, for my second cousin, back when I was about four. I was a flower girl who managed to eat more rose petals than I actually dropped. Fortunately I didn't consume my bridesmaid bouquet of chrysanthemums today.

Laura, Allie, and I wore vintage-style dresses designed by none other than the soon-to-be-famous Beanie Jacobs. The dresses were a combination of lace and beads and were really fun to wear. Allie's was this beautiful golden color that looked great with her blond hair. Mine was sort of a pumpkin color, and Laura's was a deep russet. Elise was quite pleased and said we looked like three beautiful autumn leaves. We liked the dresses so well that we plan to use them in a concert sometime.

Speaking of concerts, Allie is much better now, back in school, and we are once again practicing regularly. We even played a few of our more mellow songs for the wedding reception today. Let me tell you, it felt totally awesome to be together again. I think we sounded pretty good too.

After the wedding, Willy and Elise left Davie with Allie's grandmother so they could go on their honeymoon to the Bahamas. And Allie is staying with me, but only after Elise gave me strict orders to make sure she eats right and goes to bed on time. Believe me, I will comply. I want Allie to recover completely so we can go back on the road soon. Hopefully in time for the holiday tour that Omega is planning for Iron Cross and us.

Willy said that we'll only be doing six concerts for this tour, and Allie's doctor is pretty sure that Allie should be ready. It's reassuring to know that we'll be flying to the concert locations this time, instead of going by bus. I'm sure this will be much less exhausting for Allie—and everyone else, for that matter. Also, now that Elise and Willy are officially hitched, Elise can come along as our chaperone again. Of course, we'll miss Caitlin a lot, but we understand that she needs to continue her education. And we're already discussing the possibility of her coming with us again next summer.

After we played for the wedding reception today, Laura told me that she's ready to pick up and go tour whenever.

"I really miss it," she said. "My classes at the community college are okay and everything, but I wouldn't care if I had to just drop them, if that meant we could hit the road again."

"Yeah, I know what you mean," I said. "I'm itching to get out there too." I glanced over to where Allie was getting her picture taken with Elise and Willy and Davie. "But we've got to make sure Allie is completely well first."

Laura nodded. "I know. And I know how she feels too. I remember how I felt so bad, like it was totally my fault when our tour was jeopardized because of my problems last year. So, believe me, I'm not putting any pressure on the girl."

"Good. I guess this is just another one of those things where we have to trust God's perfect timing again." I waved over to where my brother was standing and visiting with some of his old friends, including Caitlin, who'd made a special trip home to come to the wedding.

"How does Josh like his new job?" asked Laura.

"He seems to love it. And the kids seem to love him too."

"Is it weird for you, I mean having your brother leading the youth group in your own church?"

"I think it's pretty cool."

And I really do. I was more excited than anyone when I heard that Pastor Tony had offered Josh the position after Greg took a job as the head pastor in a small church in a nearby town. The agreement is that Josh will work for a year, and then he may return to college for his master's degree. But as he keeps reminding everyone, his heart is really in the mission field. "It's not that I don't love you guys," he assured the youth group recently. "But there are so many needs out there in the rest of the world. I mean, compared to most countries, we Americans are a little spoiled."

So already the youth group is starting to plan another Mexico trip for next summer. And Redemption is planning to show up for another benefit concert too, hopefully when it's not so hot down there, although Josh said not to count on it.

"Did you know that Caitlin was one of the people who first got this whole Mexico thing going?" Josh said to me the other day.

"Huh?"

"Well, Clay Berringer had originally planned the first trip, but then he was killed in the shooting. After that Caitlin helped with some fund-raising and got people interested in Mexico, and partly because of her early involvement, it's just continued over the years." He smiled. "Isn't it amazing how one single life can make that much difference?"

And I have to agree with him there. It is amazing. It's like God has given each one of us something special and unique. Something we alone can contribute to the planet and the human condition. Something that can make a difference, maybe even change the world. And yet that something may seem small and insignificant to us, but if we trust God and use what He's given us, it might grow into something totally beyond our wildest imaginings.

SEEDS
looks like nothing
seems so small
cannot change
a thing at all
who would miss it
even care
if it wasn't
even there

but when planted
carefully
watered, tended
prayerfully
this small seed
will start to grow
it's not long
until you know
something real
is taking place
full of life
and love and grace
growing up
and growing tall
and casting seeds
to one and all
and once again
the cycle starts
seeds are planted
inside hearts
cm

Twenty-Eight

Sunday, October 23

Attention, everyone! Breaking News Report! Josh Miller has asked Caitlin O'Conner to marry him, and she said YES.

Well, of course I knew it would happen some-day, but I have to admit that it even caught me off-guard. This is how it happened. And I think the story is pretty right on since I got to hear it from both Josh and Caitlin during lunch today. Josh invited both families to join them for lunch while the two of them made their big announce-ment.

Apparently, after the wedding yesterday, Josh invited Caitlin to take a walk in the park with him (smart move on Josh's part to ensure that his "intended" was feeling romantic). Anyway, Caitlin said she thought this was a little odd since it was almost dark out and looked as if it could rain, but still she agreed. She said Josh was acting kind of strange and pretty quiet as he drove them across town, and she was actually starting to get worried, thinking maybe some-thing was seriously wrong, like he was going to tell her he had six months to live or something.

Now, I can understand her concern since Josh is usually pretty talkative.

Of course, Josh said that his silence was mainly due to fear and nerves. He didn't know if he could handle being rejected by Caitlin again. They have quite a history, you know. He said he almost decided to turn around halfway there and just forget the whole thing. But as it turned out, he had others involved, and it would've been awkward. So he drove on over to the park by the lake.

"We got out and just started to walk," said Caitlin. "The sun had gone down, and it was kind of dusky and a little on the chilly side."

"Yeah, talk about getting cold feet," said Josh. "Poor Caitlin had on these pretty shoes that were getting totally soaked from the damp grass."

She smiled at him. "Those shoes are goners now."

"But as usual, she was being a good sport," said Josh.

"Although I was wondering," continued Caitlin. "I thought something must really be wrong. I'd never seen Josh act so weird. So serious and glum. But I was afraid to ask."

"I walked her over by the docks," said Josh, eager to get this part of the story out. "You see, I'd had a couple of guys from youth group help me set this up. We had a table with a tablecloth and everything, and chairs, all set up right by the lake."

Caitlin nodded. "He even had candles and music and flowers."

"Yeah, you should've heard Caitlin," said Josh. "At first she thought we were intruding on something someone else had set up."

"Well, it just looked so strange," admitted Caitlin. "I mean, it was really pretty and everything, but it was kind of surreal. I really thought that someone else was having some sort of party and that we should walk around another way and not disturb them."

"Then I told her it was our party, and she was pretty stunned."

"Speechless." She shook her head as if she was still amazed.

"I pulled out a chair and invited her to sit," said Josh. "Then the guys, dressed like waiters, brought us our dinner that had been cooked by Alex DeBorge's mom—"

"And man, can she cook," said Caitlin. "It was amazing."

"I've heard she's quite the gourmet," my mom said, the first word anyone else had been able to get in.

"She is," said Caitlin. "I almost forgot how weird the whole thing was once I started eating her homemade linguini with pesto sauce."

"I knew that was Caitlin's favorite," said Josh.

"Well, we were almost done with the meal—"

"But we hadn't had dessert," added Josh.

"When it started to rain."

We all made compassionate sounds of empathy.

"Yeah," said Caitlin. "The candles were sputtering out, and everything was getting totally soaked."

"I didn't know what to do," said Josh. "I felt bad Caitlin was getting wet."

"So, he got out of his chair and put his coat over me," said Caitlin. "And then he got down on one knee, right there in the mud..." She looked dreamily at my brother.

"And I popped the big question," he finished.

"Let's see that ring again," said Caitlin's mom.

Caitlin held out her left hand, showing everyone the solitaire diamond that Josh had picked out the previous week—with the help of Beanie Jacobs, who had been sworn to secrecy, which she'd apparently managed to keep.

"It's exquisite," my mom said for the second time. And I know she's got good taste in jewelry so I'm guessing it's a pretty nice ring.

And so there you have it. Josh and Caitlin are engaged. They're talking about a spring wedding but haven't set an official date yet. Naturally, both sets of parents are excited and looking forward to being involved in the wedding, although I couldn't help but cringe when Mrs. O'Conner and my mom began to politely disagree over the best location for the reception. Mrs. O'Conner, who's pretty down to earth and practical, felt the church fellowship hall would be perfectly fine, but my mom, still a little stuck in her old ways, insisted the country club would be better. So it should be interesting.

I think if I ever get married (and believe me, I try not to think about this too much), I'll just elope or something. Of course, I would never tell my parents this (especially my mom), since I'm sure it would hurt their feelings. Also it probably wouldn't help Caitlin and Josh's case since then my well-meaning mom would think this is going to be her one and only big wedding.

Anyway, however it works out for Josh and Caitlin, I'm just glad they've finally figured it all out and are actually going to be married. And naturally, I offered the services of our band to perform at their reception—whether it's in the fellowship hall or the Taj Mahal!

LOVE
love that's real
between two hearts
will never end
once it starts
persevering
through the night
love will shine

in morning's light
love hangs in there
come whatever
through the storms
and rainy weather
love will bind
their hearts as one
love's good work
is never done
love knows how
to hope and wait
it defeats
both lies and hate
love endures
it runs the race
forgives, forgets
is washed in grace
cm

Twenty-Nine

Monday, December 5

We're flying to Nashville now, where the holiday tour will officially begin on Wednesday night. We have six concerts to perform in two and a half weeks. I think we're up for it. Allie says she's never felt better. But Elise insists she will be taking it easy. I think we'll all be taking it easy—in between performances, that is. I plan to take it hard and fast while we're on stage. That's who we are and what our fans expect. We can't give them less than our best.

I'm looking forward to seeing Jeremy again. I would be lying to say I wasn't. Still, I am telling myself to watch it, to keep things even keeled, to not be swept away. We've been e-mailing pretty regularly, and I think we're both on the same page in this regard. We get to admire one another from a safe distance. But oh, how I would love to wrap my arms around him and—okay, now just stop it, Chloe. Control yourself. Sigh. I guess I'm still human after all.

Fortunately, I have Laura and Allie to help keep me grounded. I know I can't get away with anything with them around. And believe me, I'm thankful for that. I love Laura and Allie so much. They feel like real flesh-and-blood sisters to me. I don't know if I will ever love any other girlfriends as much as I love those two. Okay, maybe Caitlin. And Beanie comes in a close second. I guess there's enough love to go around.

I finished up all of my tests and classes in order to graduate early. Mrs. King said they were all very impressed with the results. So I suppose this means I'm pretty much finished with high school now, although I don't feel like it. I may decide to march with the graduating class next spring after all, just so I'll know that I really made it. Or maybe not. We'll see how life goes.

Omega is already scheduling us to make another CD next April, so I guess our career is still on track. Even so, I remind myself daily that everything is in God's hands. And if all this ends tomorrow, whether I have a big old music contract or not, I will trust Him that life goes on no matter what. I can live without a lot of things, including my career in music, but I cannot live without God.

ALL I NEED
if You took
away the frills
removed the fame,
packed up the thrills
if You stripped

away the glitz
no longer welcome
at the Ritz
if all was lost
and i became
someone with no
famous name
if i were poor
as poor could be
lived on the streets
just You and me
i'd be okay
i'd be just fine
if i were Yours
and You were mine
You're all i need
my everything
You're my first love
You are my King
You are my life
You are my breath
without You, Lord
would be my death
You're all i need
You light my fire
You are my God
my one desire
amen
cm

Discussion Questions

1. As Redemption becomes more famous, the band's challenges change. What would be your biggest challenge if you suddenly became rich and famous?

2. How would you define Chloe? As a musician, composer, performer, minister, teenage girl, and Christian? Why?

3. How do you define yourself? Why?

4. Chloe was considering early graduation from high school. Do you think this was a good idea? Why or why not?

5. Chloe's relationship with her mom really improved in this book. What do you attribute that to? How is your relationship with your parents?

6. Do you think maturity is always measured in age and years? What makes a person seem mature or immature to you?

7. Chloe and Jeremy's relationship takes a big turn in this book. Do you think they handled it right? How would you handle it?

8. Chloe tries to keep her priorities with God in first place, her family and friends next, and finally her music. How do you prioritize your life?

9. Chloe is devastated by Tiffany Knight's death. How would you feel if someone you knew died? What would you wish you'd said to them before they were gone?

10. Redemption sees their music as a ministry. What do you have in your life that feels like a ministry to you? What would you like to have?

The publisher and author would love to hear your comments about this book. *Please contact us at:* www.letstalkfiction.com

THE DIARY OF A TEENAGE GIRL SERIES
ENTER CHLOE'S WORLD

MY NAME IS CHLOE, Chloe book one

Chloe Miller, Josh's younger sister, is a free spirit with dramatic clothes and hair. She struggles with her own identity, classmates, parents, boys, and—whether or not God is for real. But this unconventional high school freshman definitely doesn't hold back when she meets Him in a big, personal way. Chloe expresses God's love and grace through the girl band she forms, Redemption, and continues to show the world she's not willing to conform to anyone else's image of who or what she should be. Except God's, that is.

ISBN 1-59052-018-1

SOLD OUT, Chloe book two

Chloe and her fellow band members must sort out their lives as they become a hit in the local community. And after a talent scout from Nashville discovers the trio, all too soon their explosive musical ministry begins to encounter conflicts with family, so-called friends, and school. Exhilarated yet frustrated, Chloe puts her dream in God's hand and prays for Him to work out the details.

ISBN 1-59052-141-2

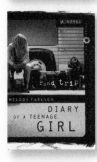

ROAD TRIP, Chloe book three

After signing with a major record company, Redemption's dreams are coming true. Chloe, Allie, and Laura begin their concert tour with the good-looking guys in the band Iron Cross. But as soon as the glitz and glamour wear off, the girls find life on the road a little overwhelming. Even rock solid Laura appears to be feeling the stress—and Chloe isn't quite sure how to confront her about the growing signs of drug addiction...

ISBN 1-59052-142-0

FACE THE MUSIC, Chloe book four

Redemption has made it to the bestseller chart, but what Chloe and the girls need most is some downtime to sift through the usual high school stress with grades, friends, guys, and the prom. Chloe struggles to recover from a serious crush on the band leader of Iron Cross. Then just as an unexpected romance catches Redemption by surprise, Caitlin O'Conner—whose relationship with Josh is taking on a new dimension—joins the tour as their chaperone. Chloe's wild ride only speeds up, and this one-of-a-kind musician faces the fact that life may never be normal again.

ISBN 1-59052-241-9

THE DIARY OF A TEENAGE GIRL SERIES
ENTER CAITLIN'S WORLD

DIARY OF A TEENAGE GIRL, Caitlin book one

Follow sixteen-year-old Caitlin O'Conner as she makes her way through life—surviving a challenging home life, school pressures, an identity crisis, and the uncertainties of "true love." You'll cry with Caitlin as she experiences heartache, and cheer for her as she encounters a new reality in her life: God. See how rejection by one group can—incredibly—sometimes lead you to discover who you really are.

ISBN 1-57673-735-7

IT'S MY LIFE, Caitlin book two

Caitlin faces new trials as she strives to maintain the recent commitments she's made to God. Torn between new spiritual directions and loyalty to Beanie, her pregnant best friend, Caitlin searches out her personal values on friendship, dating, life goals, and family.

ISBN 1-59052-053-X

WHO I AM, Caitlin book three

As a high school senior, Caitlin's relationship with Josh takes on a serious tone via e-mail—threatening her commitment to "kiss dating goodbye." When Beanie begins dating an African-American, Caitlin's concern over dating seems to be misread as racism. One thing is obvious: God is at work through this dynamic girl in very real but puzzling ways, and a soul-stretching time of racial reconciliation at school and within her church helps her discover God's will as never before.

ISBN 1-57673-890-6

ON MY OWN, Caitlin book four

An avalanche of emotion hits Caitlin as she lands at college and begins to realize she's not in high school anymore. Buried in course-work and far from her best friend, Beanie, Caitlin must cope with her new roommate's bad attitude, manic music, and sleazy social life. Should she have chosen a Bible college like Josh? Maybe...but how to survive the year ahead is the big question right now!

ISBN 1-59052-017-3

Visit

www.letstalkfiction.com

today!

Fiction Readers Unite!

Y ou've just found a new way to feed your fiction addiction. Letstalkfiction.com is a place where fiction readers can come together to learn about new fiction releases from Multnomah. You can read about the latest book releases, catch a behind-the-scenes look at your favorite authors, sign up to receive the most current book information, and much more. Everything you need to make the most out of your fictional world can be found at www.letstalkfiction.com. Come and join the network!

HEY, GOD, WHAT DO YOU WANT FROM ME?

More and more teens find themselves growing up in a world lacking in godly wisdom and direction. In *Piercing Proverbs,* bestselling youth fiction author Melody Carlson offers solid messages of the Bible in a version that can compete with TV, movies, and the Internet for the attention of this vital group in God's kingdom. Choosing life-impacting portions of teen-applicable Proverbs, Carlson paraphrases them into understandable, teen-friendly language and presents them as guidelines for clearly identified areas of life (such as friendship, family, money, and mistakes). Teens will easily read and digest these high-impact passages of the Bible delivered in their own words.

ISBN 1-57673-895-7